'You misunderstand,' he said abruptly. 'The ransom wasn't money; it was the Peacock's Eye.'

'I've heard of that,' she said slowly. 'It's jewellery, isn't it?'

'It's jewellery,' Rafiq agreed wryly. The Eye was a dazzling necklace, ancient and heavy with the weight of solid gold and gems, designed to mimic the pattern on a peacock's tail feather. Its value was in its magnificent wealth: the huge emeralds alone were beyond price. But much more important was its historic and cultural significance to Q'aroum.

'But, more than that, it's an heirloom that holds unique significance in our heritage. For generations it's been the traditional gift of the royal Sheikh to his bride.'

Her jaw dropped.

'According to the custom of my people,' he continued, 'since I relinquished it in return for you, I've paid it as a bride price. Which means that as far as Q'aroum is concerned, Belle, you are my affianced bride.'

Annie West spent her childhood with her nose between the covers of a book—a habit she retains. After years preparing government reports and official correspondence, she decided to write something she *really* enjoys. And there's nothing she loves more than a great romance. Despite her office-bound past she has managed a few interesting moments—including a marriage offer with the promise of a herd of camels to sweeten the contract. She is happily married to her ever-patient husband (who has never owned a dromedary). They live with their two children amongst the tall eucalypts at beautiful Lake Macquarie, on Australia's east coast.

Recent titles by the same author:

THE GREEK'S CONVENIENT MISTRESS
A MISTRESS FOR THE TAKING

THE SHEIKH'S
RANSOMED BRIDE

BY
ANNIE WEST

MILLS & BOON®

All the characters in this book have no existence outside the imagination of the author, and have no relation whatsoever to anyone bearing the same name or names. They are not even distantly inspired by any individual known or unknown to the author, and all the incidents are pure invention.

First published in Great Britain 2007
Harlequin Mills & Boon Limited,
Eton House, 18-24 Paradise Road, Richmond, Surrey TW9 1SR

© Annie West 2007

ISBN-13: 978 0 263 85315 5
ISBN-10:   0 263 85315 2

Set in Times Roman 10¼ on 12¼ pt
01-0407-52971

Printed and bound in Spain
by Litografia Rosés, S.A., Barcelona

THE SHEIKH'S
RANSOMED
BRIDE

Once again—thank you, Karen,
especially for those long discussions on the mystique
of the sheikh story. What an inspiration they were.

Thanks as well to Heather, Judy and Kez for the
comments, and to Mary, Tan, Lisa and most especially
Lea for your enthusiasm. No hero could have a
better welcoming committee!

CHAPTER ONE

BELLE clasped her hands tight together and concentrated on not being scared.

The rough floor was hard beneath her weary body, making her wish she wore something more than a swimsuit. The unforgiving rasp of iron around the chafed skin of her wrists and ankles was bearable if she didn't move.

But she couldn't dispel the acrid taste of fear on her tongue. Or the brutal images of violence that replayed in her mind.

Shivering, she looked down at Duncan. Her colleague was pale, but mercifully asleep on the narrow pallet. She'd splinted his leg as best she could, and the bleeding had stopped. There wasn't anything more she could do for him.

Except pray.

She'd done little else for thirty hours. Since their kidnappers had dumped them here: not merely isolated in this ramshackle hut, but the only people on the whole blisteringly hot islet.

Yesterday she'd explored, scouring it for anything they could use to summon help or to escape. She couldn't have missed anything. She'd had to crawl on her hands and knees since the heavy shackles had kept tripping her up.

If she'd been able to walk properly she'd have circled the island in five minutes. A bare atoll: sand, a couple of palm trees and this ruined hut. No help. No supplies.

Unwillingly she let her gaze stray to the single large water bottle their captors had left behind. She hadn't tasted water since sunrise, knowing Duncan needed it more. Now the bottle was perilously close to empty. Her tongue was thick and swollen from dehydration. Had they been left to die? Her empty stomach cramped savagely at the thought.

None of this made sense. Not the abduction from their dive-boat nor their abandonment. She and Duncan weren't typical kidnap victims. They weren't rich or powerful. They hadn't offended local sensibilities with their survey of a sunken first-century trading ship. Everyone in Q'aroum had been so friendly and helpful.

Belle chewed her lip, trying not to dwell on the possibility that two marine archaeologists might die of thirst before they could be rescued. The Arabian Sea was vast, and this island so tiny it wouldn't be on a map.

Would they be back, those brutal men who'd looked as if they'd enjoy nothing better than slitting her throat?

Even with masks hiding their faces, she'd known they wouldn't hesitate to kill. There'd been callous excitement in their hard, glittering eyes. Sadistic enjoyment of their victims' desperate fear.

Belle shuddered and blinked her gritty eyes against scalding tears of fury and fright. She would *not* give in to panic. Her only hope, hers and Duncan's, was to be strong. To concentrate on staying alive. No matter what the odds.

Deliberately she turned her thoughts to her family in Australia. She drew strength from the knowledge that, if she survived this ordeal, her mum and sister would be waiting for her.

When, she reminded herself, not *if* she escaped.

Belle pressed her palms to her aching eyes, ignoring the burn of unshed tears against her lids. She hadn't slept and exhaustion sapped her strength. She couldn't stop shaking. She slumped, fighting the despair that welled up inside her, clogging her throat and weighting her heart.

Gingerly she settled herself on the floor. She wouldn't sleep, but she needed to recruit her strength.

Reluctantly she closed her eyes.

The noise woke her. A yowling wail that tore through the air and made the roof groan. They were in for a storm.

Belle opened her eyes and realised where she was. And that they weren't alone any more.

Her heart thudded frantically, the sound of it swelling to a deafening roar in her ears. Her parched throat closed as she watched a man bend over Duncan. A torch propped on the floor illuminated the puckered scar that lined the man's cheek and ran up to his short grizzled hair. A large gun was slung over his shoulder, and on the floor beside his boot she saw a long, curved blade. The Middle Eastern version of a Bowie-knife.

He reached out a hand towards Duncan's throat, and Belle knew with terrified certainty that she had to act fast. Her colleague was in no state to save himself.

And yet she had to force herself to move. Dread was a physical weight pushing down on her. She knew she had no hope against the stranger.

Her stiff muscles screamed in protest as she shifted, centimetre by centimetre, till her fingers closed on the knife handle. It was heavy, smooth and well worn. Her arm wobbled as she lifted its deadly weight in her damp hands.

The intruder grabbed Duncan's neck, and in that instant Belle struggled to her knees, unsteady but determined. Her clumsy movement took their gaoler by surprise, and she thrust the wicked blade against his neck. He froze.

'Move and you're dead,' she snarled, her voice a raw, broken whisper.

For a moment there was stillness.

Then out of the darkness a large hand clamped onto hers. Fingers strong as a vice closed on her, shutting off the circulation till her hands throbbed.

But she wouldn't let go. The knife was all she had to protect them.

'Quiet, little tigress.' The voice came out of the gloom, deep and mellifluous. 'We're friends: here to help.'

Turning her head towards the voice, she saw the gleam of eyes close to hers. Now she felt the heat of his body too. She shivered at the sensation of power that emanated from him.

The pressure of his fingers strengthened just a fraction and she cried out. The knife clattered to the floor as stars exploded across her vision.

Immediately he released his grip, and blood pounded agonisingly into her fingers. She bit down on her lip, cradling her hands against her chest as she blinked back scalding tears of pain and fear and frustration.

There was a scraping noise, and the man who'd threatened Duncan scuttled out of reach, taking the knife.

The man at her side grabbed the torch, and she winced as light dazzled her. The beam swung down to illuminate her hands. There was a hiss of indrawn breath from across the room. And from beside her came the soft sound of swearing, furious and unmistakable, in unintelligible Arabic.

The light moved on, flicking over her briefly but comprehensively. Then, mercifully, he put the torch on the floor, tilted once more towards Duncan, who still slept.

'It's all right, Ms Winters.' The man with the deep voice spoke again. Now she detected the hint of a lilting accent in his precise tones. 'We're here to rescue you.'

Rescue! Her head spun and she slumped back on her heels. Could it be true? She struggled to take it in.

A hand, large and warm, settled on her arm.

'You'll be all right while we look after your friend?'

She nodded. 'I'm OK,' she croaked.

He said something to his companion, who returned to squat beside the pallet, reaching out to Duncan. Now she realised he was searching for a pulse. A flood of relief washed over her as she realised it was true. These strangers were here to rescue them.

'Drink this.' The man who appeared to be the leader of the pair held a canteen to her dry lips, tilting it so she could swallow a welcome trickle. Greedily she raised her hands to the canteen, tipping it further. Sweet water filled her mouth, ran down her burning throat.

'Steady,' he warned. 'Too much and you'll be sick.'

She knew he was right. But she was desperate for more. It was only his unbreakable hold on the water bottle that prevented her from guzzling.

'That's enough.' His low voice burred near her ear.

If she'd had the strength she might have complained about his high-handedness. But her attack on his companion had used her last reserves of strength. She swayed drunkenly to one side.

Immediately the stranger put his big hands on her shoulders to steady her. Calluses scraped her bare sunburnt flesh and she flinched. He cursed again.

'I'm sorry,' she mumbled. 'I'm a bit unsteady.'

'It's a wonder you're even conscious.' His voice was harsh but his hands were gentle. 'Here.' He pulled her towards him, taking her weight easily.

She had a brief impression of heat and strength. A tantalising awareness of some unfamiliar scent: sun and salt and man. Then he lowered her onto a cotton blanket. 'Lie still while we see how Mr MacDonald is.'

'You know our names?' she whispered.

'It's not often we have kidnappings in Q'aroum. Much less

the abduction of two foreign nationals. Of course we know who you are.' His voice was grim. 'There's been a co-ordinated air and sea search for the pair of you ever since your boatman reported the abduction.'

He brushed her tangled hair back from her face and she shut her eyes, feeling absurdly close to tears at the tender gesture.

'Rest now,' he murmured, and she sensed him move away.

She ached in every joint, and her throat was as painfully dry as the hot wind that swooped south towards them off the Arabian Peninsula. Her head pounded and she knew she'd reached the limit of her endurance.

But there was soft fabric against her cheek and under her body. And the caress of that big calloused hand had invested her with hope again. Hope and reassurance. She recalled his voice, low and velvety. Her body had tingled into feminine awareness at the sound of it, despite the extremity of her situation.

If this was a hallucination she didn't want it to end. She could drift off happily now, resigned to her fate.

She may even have dozed. The low murmur from the two men as they investigated Duncan's injuries was as soothing as the sound of waves lapping on a beach.

She frowned, registering through the muddled haze of her thoughts that the wind was still picking up. Palm fronds slapped against the roof and there was a dull roar in the distance, like a freight train heading towards them.

Opening her eyes, she looked blearily at the strangers. A second powerful torch added light to the scene. She recognised the pattern of desert-coloured camouflage gear and heavy boots. Army? Or perhaps mercenaries? Right now she didn't care, as long as they were here to rescue them. Then the guy with the grey hair moved to one side, and she sucked in an astonished breath as she saw the second man in the light for the first time.

She'd been rescued by a pirate!

Belle shut her eyes, realising it was some trick of the light and her tired brain. But when she opened them to stare again there was no mistake.

His black hair was combed back ruthlessly, revealing a fighter's grim face: one of stark, slashing lines. Despite its severity his was one of the most breathtaking faces she'd ever seen. Every inch was hard and uncompromising, from his long, commanding nose to his solid jaw and the deep grooves bracketing his mouth. Every inch except for that mouth, which in repose spoke of sensual knowledge.

The angle of the torch highlighted the fanning lines at the corners of his eyes: the telltale sign of a man who spent his hours outdoors in this hot climate.

But, despite his army issue gear, the man deftly bandaging Duncan's leg to a professional-looking splint was definitely in no one's army. A heavy-looking hoop of gold caught the light at one earlobe as he moved. And behind his head she glimpsed hair pulled back in a ponytail. Absolutely not army regulation.

Abruptly he raised his face to meet her gaze, and she sucked in a stunned breath. For a long moment they watched each other. Long enough for her to imagine a pulse of something hot and knowing in his eyes.

He looked like a buccaneer who'd just spied a trophy ship.

She swallowed at the frisson of something very like fear, staring back into his ruthless face.

Abruptly he gave an order to his companion, who moved immediately to her side, holding out the canteen. It was only as she reached gratefully for it that the leader of the pair looked away, and she felt the tension that had spun tight round her dissipate.

She propped herself up on an elbow and drank, careful this time to take it slowly. The man with the scarred face nodded approvingly and murmured something encouraging. He too looked as if he belonged on a tall-masted ship where the rules of civilised society didn't apply.

Hell! She must be weaker than she'd thought. Maybe heat and stress and lack of water were making her delusional.

One of her rescuers looked like a typecast villain, and the other as if he'd stepped out of some swashbuckling fantasy. It had to be a trick of the poor light.

Reluctantly she handed back the water bottle, then let her head sink to the cushioning blanket. Soon, perhaps in a few hours, she'd be back in the Kingdom of Q'aroum, receiving the best of modern medical attention.

The two men packed their medical supplies. And still Duncan slept. 'Is he all right?' There was a telltale quiver of fear in her voice that brought the buccaneer's gaze up to meet hers.

'It's a bad fracture,' he replied. 'And he's lost a lot of blood. But he should recover quickly once we get him to hospital.' His eyes narrowed. 'He doesn't seem to be dehydrated. You've done a good job looking after him.'

And not such a good job looking after yourself, his stare seemed to say. But what else could she have done? Drunk all the water and left Duncan in need?

'He's still asleep,' she said. 'Or unconscious?' Surely the pain of bandaging his leg should have woken him?

'I've given your colleague a strong painkiller that's knocked him out for the moment. It's best if he doesn't wake while we move him.'

Belle nodded, knowing he was right. But she'd be relieved to see Duncan conscious again. He'd drifted in and out of delirium for too long now.

She watched, heavy-eyed, as the men conferred in Arabic. The older one, with the scar, pointed to Duncan and herself. And all the while the wind gusted and swirled, making the shack's walls creak and the roof shudder. Then the conversation was over. The younger man spoke once, decisively, and it seemed they were in agreement.

They turned to the hut's rough wooden door, working together: the older one heavy-set and methodical, the younger man lithe but broad-shouldered and strong. It only took a few minutes to get the door off. Then they laid it beside the pallet, ignoring the whirling gusts that hurled sand through the gaping doorway.

Of course. It was a makeshift stretcher for Duncan.

Time she got ready. Carefully Belle inched herself up, wincing as she scraped her chafed ankles. By the time she had manoeuvred herself to her knees, ready to rise, she was breathless, and pain thrummed in her hands and feet.

'What are you doing?' That deep voice was dangerously low, sending a thread of renewed tension spidering up her backbone. She looked up as he loomed over her, a tall pirate. In the shadows she could see his sensuous mouth was a taut line. His brow furrowed.

'I'm getting ready to leave.' Obviously.

'Not yet.'

'But I—'

'It will take two of us to get Mr MacDonald to the boat. I can't look after you and carry him.'

'I don't need looking after!' She'd survived this long virtually alone. She could make it to the boat by herself. All she wanted was to get off this godforsaken island. After what she'd been through, scrambling to the shore would be a doddle. She wouldn't feel completely safe till she'd left this prison behind.

He hunkered down in front of her, blocking off the torchlight so she couldn't read his features. But she felt his warm breath on her face. Inhaled the spicy scent of his skin.

Somewhere low in her abdomen a quiver of excitement flared.

'You're hurt, Ms Winters.' His tone was patient. Almost.

'You've done everything you could in the circumstances. Now it's time to let us take care of you.'

It made sense. Even to someone as desperate to escape as she was. Reluctantly she nodded.

'Good.' He reached for the blanket and draped it over her shoulders, pulling it round her as protection against the grit laden wind. She winced at the abrasion of cloth against tender skin.

'I'll leave a torch,' he said, placing it so its light shone towards the door. 'And I'll be back soon.'

Then they disappeared into the howling darkness, carrying Duncan. Leaving her to wonder who they were.

Or, more precisely, who *he* was. The man with a voice like a caress. If it weren't for that hint of an accent she'd have thought him English. Well-educated English. But he was probably local. His deep olive complexion was the norm in the Arab world.

Not that Q'aroum was a typical Arab country. As a fiercely independent island nation in the Arabian Sea, it had been home for centuries to adventurers and buccaneers from the Middle East, Africa and beyond.

The proud tilt of his head, the way he walked, as if he owed allegiance to no man, made her think of long ago princes. Or pirates.

She really had to find a new fantasy, she decided wearily as she pulled the blanket closer, huddling into its comfort. If only it could block out the lashing sand and the sound of the rising storm. Experience told her this was no minor gale. This was seriously nasty weather. And she wanted to be back on the main island when it hit.

It took a moment for her to realise he was back, his approach hidden by the storm. She raised her eyes from his boots all the way up to his face as he stood in the doorway.

His expression was unreadable, but his watchfulness and the way he obviously masked his thoughts made her shiver.

There was something wrong. She could feel it.

'What is it?' she whispered as fear clawed its way back up her throat, drying her mouth once more.

The torchlight cast heavy shadows on his face, emphasising the compelling personality she sensed in him. This time it didn't reassure.

He moved into the room, pacing slowly towards her in a way that made her shrink back a little under her covering. He stopped, folded his legs beneath him and, in a single supple motion, sat cross-legged in front of her.

'There's a complication to our plans,' he said.

Belle swallowed hard as apprehension shivered through her. She didn't want to hear this. She looked into his gleaming eyes and tried to draw on his strength. She wasn't alone any more. Whatever it was, she would cope.

'What's the problem?'

'Dawud and I came over on an inflatable,' he explained. 'It's a small boat.'

She nodded impatiently. She knew inflatables.

'No,' he said. 'I mean this one is *small*. Too small for all four of us now that Mr MacDonald is strapped across the length of it.'

'I see.' The disappointment was so strong she felt like weeping. Ridiculous, since all she had to do was wait for Dawud to come back to collect them.

Patience, Belle. Just a little longer.

'Well, we'll just have to wait for Dawud to return.'

He paused for a second before shaking his head. 'I'm afraid it's not that simple.'

She really had a bad feeling about this now. Foreboding sliced through her. She hunched lower under the protection of her blanket.

'There's a storm coming this way. A cyclone.' His voice was steady, unemotional.

Her heart plunged and her hands clamped, white-knuckled with effort as she willed herself not to shake.

'Dawud's left. He should just have time to reach port before it becomes too dangerous. But it would be suicide for him or anyone else to return tonight.' The buccaneer scrutinised her, as if watching for signs of weakness. 'We'll be stranded here until the storm passes. Maybe for another twenty-four hours.'

Twenty-four hours. It sounded like a lifetime.

And, if the cyclone hit head-on, time enough to die.

She felt sick with disappointment after the certainty she'd been rescued. Nausea welled and she swallowed hard, oblivious now to the raw abrasiveness of her throat.

At least Duncan had got away safely.

Belle stared at the man before her. His gaze was impenetrable and his utter stillness gave nothing away. Neither urgency nor the fear that would be natural in the circumstances. The fear that froze her own limbs right now.

But something about the set of his shoulders, the casual grace of his hands resting at his folded knees, told her he was ready for anything, even a hysterical woman.

She gnawed at her lip, willing the trembling to subside. She'd seen tropical cyclones as a kid on the Great Barrier Reef coast. She knew how devastating they were. Involuntarily she looked up at the barely-there roof. It shifted and groaned in the gale. 'How can we prepare?'

He inclined his head and the waiting stillness left his body. As if she'd passed some test. He'd expected her to panic, had braced himself to handle a distraught woman.

He gestured to her blanket. 'If you'll permit?' When she nodded he folded it back to reveal her bare feet. She shuddered as the torchlight illuminated her, and she felt a ridiculous urge to tuck her feet back out of sight.

They were filthy with sand and dried blood. Each ankle

ringed with red welts where the shackles had bitten into her skin as she moved.

In the gloom his face was impassive. Yet she read tension in his clamped jaw as he surveyed her injuries. And the air between them was electric, charged with some fierce emotion that radiated from him in waves.

Anger? Or frustration that he had this to deal with as well as the approaching storm?

She shrank further under her cotton wrap as she felt his eyes on her face. She wished she could read his expression. Instinct warned her to be wary of this man. It was crazy. She had to trust him. He was risking his life for her, a stranger. What danger could she be in from him?

Despite the fine, dusty sand swirling around them Belle could identify what had to be his own natural scent: clean male skin with a slight salt tang. She shivered.

'Shouldn't you release my hands first?' Then she could help strengthen the shelter. And she'd be less dependent on him. She'd feel better if she could help herself.

'Later. It's important that your legs are free.'

Why? They had nowhere to go. And with the sea churning in the strong winds the surface of their atoll could only get smaller. It was only a couple of metres above sea level—that was nothing if the cyclone hit them full-force.

The truth was sudden and horrifying.

He must have sensed the immediate tension in her. He looked up, his eyes darkly gleaming. 'Are you all right?'

Oh, she was just dandy. Wearily she inclined her head. Now she understood his reasoning. 'It'll be easier to swim with the shackles off,' she said. 'If we get swamped.'

He shifted, and the torchlight glanced off his strongly honed features. It revealed a calm certainty and a strength that, beyond all reason, reassured.

'I will look after you,' he said slowly. 'I promise you.' It sounded like a pledge. In that moment she had no doubt he'd give his all to save her.

But would that be enough to preserve either of them?

'Have faith, Ms Winters,' he said in a steady voice. 'I will see you through this. The eye of the storm is predicted to track further west. It will be unpleasant here, but we will survive it—together. Now, sit still while I do my best with the lock.'

He spread a small packet of tools beside him. Then one large, warm hand cupped her heel and she sucked in a stunned breath as her reeling senses reacted to his touch. It was impersonal, she assured herself, merely steadying her foot to give him better access to the heavy shackles.

But she couldn't ignore the tiny, trembling waves of awareness that spread up her leg. Reaction to her ordeal. That was what it was. No man, no matter how starkly sexy, had the power to generate electricity with his bare hands.

She shut her eyes to block out the image of his dark head bent low over her, the light gilding the aristocratic ridge of his cheekbone and glinting on the barbaric-looking ring at his ear.

The gale roared around their refuge and the air swirled, heavy with grit, presaging the devastation fast approaching. Yet tucked in this corner, her world limited to the scope of a torch beam, she felt cocooned in a fragile, dream-like world. Protected by this remarkable man.

Remarkable? She didn't know anything about him except for his extraordinary good looks. And his palpable aura of authority. The sense that he would cope: not just survive, but triumph, no matter what the odds.

A jarring movement broke her reverie and she opened her eyes. He'd attempted to pick the lock. Blood covered his wrist from a long gash—his hold must have slipped.

'Are you all right?'

He raised his head and she could have sworn she saw a flash of humour lurking in his eyes. But he didn't laugh at the absurdity of her, trussed before him like a sacrificial victim, worrying about his injury. 'I'll live.'

The chain at her feet jolted, then blessedly gave way. Relief washed through her. Without the shackles wearing her down she had a slim chance of staying afloat.

Now he did smile. A dazzling grin that lit the uncompromising angles of his face into a less austere, but still riveting male beauty. Dazed, Belle's eyes widened. She'd thought him sexy before. Now he was simply stunning.

No real-life pirate had ever looked that good!

'Your patience has been rewarded,' he said, dropping the metal to the floor. 'And just in time.' The rain had arrived, a thunderous downpour that swept in through the door and gushed through the holes in the roof. Belle shivered as her covering grew wet. The wind was notching up too. Soon they wouldn't be able to hear each other.

'My hands…' He shook his head and held up the discarded lock. The tool he'd used had broken, jammed in the rusty metal.

Hope died in her breast, flattened by the solid weight of despair. Would she ever escape this nightmare? It grew worse and worse by the hour.

'No time,' he said as he hefted the torch, directing its beam upwards. It played over the roof that heaved like a living thing. And then the bulging walls.

She heard a whisper of a curse from the man before her. Then he was on his feet, shouldering his backpack.

He loomed before her, big and solid. She caught a glimpse of his determined face before he bent and the light went out. Then his hands were on her, pulling her up. 'Lift your arms,' he said in her ear.

She felt the brush of his hair against her arms. He pulled her wrists so that she strained up against him, her arms encircling his head. Then he lifted her in a single easy movement, tucking her close. A wall of solid muscle supported her, warmed her. Strong arms bound her and she sank gratefully into him, finding comfort in his strength and the steady, calming rhythm of his heart.

Despite the roar of the storm, the living pulse of the waves smashing on the shore, she could almost believe nothing bad would happen while she was with him.

'It's not safe here,' he shouted over the screeching wind. 'Hold on tight.' He turned and strode out through the door.

And then the storm swallowed them.

CHAPTER TWO

THE maelstrom buffeted them, almost knocking him to the ground. How he managed to steer a course for whatever shelter he'd found, she couldn't imagine. But his arms held her in a grip of steel as if he'd never let her go.

She buried her head into the base of his neck, shielding herself from the stinging sand. His skin was wet, slick, and scented with something she suspected was unique to him. The heavy thump of his heart, regular and strong, tempered the fear that crowded in on her.

He lowered her on her back into what felt like a hollow in the sand. As she settled in the dip he lay down above her. He was taller, broader, more solid than she. He covered her completely, a barrier against the terrifying wind that roared through the night. It was difficult to draw breath with him pressing down on her. Sand clogged her nostrils and her breathing came in rapid pants. She had to calm herself, slow her breathing.

She had to get free. She moved to slide her hands over his head. Immediately one large hand clamped hers.

'Leave them.' His lips brushed her ear. 'Less likely to be separated.'

The wind escalated to a scream, and through the din she thought she heard another sound, a heavy thud beside them.

The man above her flinched and sagged onto her, heavier than before. For a moment he was limp, squashing her down into the sand. Then he gathered himself and lifted his torso just enough so she could breathe again.

'Are you all right?' she yelled in his ear.

'Just hold on tight, Ms Winters.'

The formality was absurd in the circumstances. He was all that stood between her and possible death. This stranger who'd appeared when she was at her weakest: injured, desperate and almost despairing. He'd shared his strength, giving her hope when she most needed it.

And now, wearing nothing but a swimsuit and a pair of manacles, she lay as close to him as any lover. His bulk pressed down on her—a shield against the storm's savage fury. In the process she was discovering the unique imprint of his body, learning the impressively hard planes and lean muscles of this superbly built stranger.

And she didn't even know who he was.

She opened her mouth to ask his name, then shut it. He wouldn't be able to hear her over the tumult.

Instead she did what little she could for the man who risked his life for her. She spread her fingers over the back of his head, hoping to protect him from flying debris. Then she turned her face towards his, finding primitive comfort in the haze of his breath against her skin.

Rafiq felt the moment she surrendered to the inevitable and lay quiet beneath him. The rapid beat of her heart slowed to something closer to normal and her fierce rigidity lessened. But she didn't relax her hold. Her hands splayed protectively over his skull, as if to ward off hurt.

His lips twisted at the absurdity of the gesture.

Ms Isabelle Margaret Winters, twenty-five, of Cairns,

Australia, was a remarkable woman. A fighter, determined to push herself beyond the limits of normal endurance if she had to. She didn't give up, no matter what the odds.

She'd even tackled Dawud with his own knife!

He smiled at the memory. If they got out of this alive he'd enjoy using that piece of information.

Dawud was an old friend, but sometimes he forgot that he couldn't make Rafiq's decisions. He'd even tried to argue that *he* should stay behind with Isabelle Winters. Dawud should have known better. Rafiq was responsible for her. He knew his duty. He'd learned early to shoulder his responsibilities and face every challenge head-on.

He shifted his weight, trying to ease the searing pain in his shoulder where something had sheared through the air and slammed into him. The movement only made him more aware of her soft body cushioning him. With her arms over his shoulders, her high breasts tilted against him. Her hips cradled him in a way that made him think of bedroom pleasures. The intimate touch of her lips against his chin made him wonder what her kisses would be like.

He was aware of her with every sense. Could feel her femininity against his hardness. Despite the grit in his nostrils, he inhaled the intriguing scent of her skin. Could imagine the taste of her on his tongue.

And he could sense her confusion and desperate fear.

He dragged his brain back to their predicament, furious at his weakness. To be distracted by a beautiful woman now, in this extremity! It was beyond all logic.

Would flying debris be the worst they'd have to endure? Or would the atoll be washed away?

It was in the hands of destiny.

The thought made him recall his grandfather. The old man had firmly believed in the force of destiny. Even when he'd lost his son, Rafiq's father, he'd remained as proud and stiff-necked as ever, saying that his son's fate had been written and blaming no one for the accident.

If the old man were alive, he'd say it was Rafiq's fate to be on this outlying isle with Isabelle Winters.

After all, she wouldn't be here but for Rafiq. He'd made it his business to approve personally the members of the marine survey expedition, expediting visa arrangements. Without his agreement she wouldn't be in his country.

And now this. Guilt seared him. She was an innocent pawn in a political scheme of which she knew nothing.

The storm would delay Dawud's return to the main island. He wouldn't arrive before the deadline for payment of the kidnap ransom. And Dawud couldn't send a message ahead from the inflatable with news. The radio was dead. A malfunction due to the storm or to sabotage?

Without word that the captives were safe, no one would dare countermand Rafiq's initial order to pay the ransom if the hostages weren't found in time.

Much as it had galled him to give in to the demand, Rafiq had known immediately that Isabelle Winters and her companion were in great peril. He knew who was behind the kidnapping. And he knew that without the ransom one or both hostages would be killed.

He refused to have that on his conscience.

He'd bring the ringleader to justice. But it would be too late to save the kidnap victims. So he'd bargained for time. Q'aroum didn't need the international notoriety that the kidnap and execution of foreign nationals would bring. His country had a reputation for stability, for being a place where it was safe to do business. That couldn't be jeopardised.

So right about now, according to his instructions, the outrageous ransom demand was being paid. And there'd be no keeping it secret. Not in a place like Q'aroum, where news spread with the speed and inevitability of the desert wind.

By morning the whole island nation would know that the Peacock's Eye, the most revered and coveted family heirloom in the world, and one of his country's national treasures, had been paid for the life of the woman in his arms.

Belle woke to the dull pounding of the surf.

So. She was alive.

Experimentally she shifted her legs, gritting her teeth as abrasive sand scratched the raw skin of her ankles. Fiery circlets of pain ringed her feet, throbbing in time with her pulse.

At least she *had* a pulse. Last night she'd wondered if she'd see another dawn.

If it hadn't been for *him* she might not have survived. He'd protected her with his body as the cyclone tore the night apart. The din had stunned her, and nothing had existed beyond the barrage of sound and his weight on her. And the steady beat of his heart that had kept her hope alive.

Who was he? Where was he?

She squinted up through gritty eyes. A stab of bright sunlight blinded her and the ache in her head ignited into a flame of agony that kept time with the pulse of pain in her legs. Tentatively she moved her hands. Sharp pins and needles shot through her. She'd spent the night with her arms wrapped around his head. Now her shoulders had set.

Belle clenched her jaw as she dragged down protesting arms, rolled over and levered herself up onto her knees. Her bones had surely calcified, unwilling to permit movement. She braced herself on her hands and opened her eyes again. Blearily she focussed on the ugly manacles.

She remembered the hulking brute who'd locked them round

her wrists. His satisfaction as he'd watched her struggle against their unforgiving weight.

Suddenly she understood with nauseating certainty that lack of funds hadn't prevented the kidnappers using modern, light-weight handcuffs. Those men had bristled with an arsenal of automatic weapons. The manacles had been a deliberately sadistic choice. Anger surged through her. Searing fury at her helpless sense of violation.

But they hadn't won. She hadn't given up fighting.

She forced herself to stand, ignoring the silent scream of protesting muscles. For a moment she swayed. Then she planted her feet wide, found her balance and straightened. She narrowed her eyes against the glare. A black bank of cloud marked the distant horizon, but overhead the grey was broken by patches of bright light.

The sea was high, rough and threatening. The island wasn't familiar any more. Its boundaries had changed in the night, reshaped by the gouging sea. Slowly she turned. During the night the force of the wind and water had eaten into the island, carving a sheltered, almost enclosed inlet at its centre.

There! Was that where the hut had stood? She shuddered as she saw the remnants. It had collapsed, a death trap of tumbled walls that would have crushed anyone inside.

Her next desperate breath bruised her lungs. Her eyes swam and she stumbled. Frantically she scanned the debris for any shape that looked human.

Something dropped hard in the pit of her stomach at the possibility he might be injured. Or worse.

Slowly she turned.

And there he was.

Her unsteady legs gave way and she collapsed abruptly onto the sun-warmed sand. Her eyes widened in disbelief.

He rose like some bronzed deity from the water. Naked. Elementally masculine. Potently desirable.

Her pulse thumped a rapid tattoo in her throat and a spiral of feminine excitement coiled tight within her, making her gasp at its intensity. Thank goodness he had his back to her and couldn't read her stunned reaction.

She'd watched him in the wavering torchlight. She'd spent the night clasped in his arms, learning at first hand the tough masculine planes and bunched muscles that comprised his body. But still she hadn't been prepared.

His wide shoulders tapered through a strong torso to a lean waist. Slick jet-black hair splayed down over his neck and reached his shoulders. His skin was smooth and glistening. Belle's fingers clenched into tight fists.

Her gaze strayed lower. The curve of tight, round buttocks. The weight of muscled thighs. Innate strength and endurance. He stretched his arms out and she stared, mesmerised, at the movement of muscles in his back.

He dropped his hands to his sides and shook his head, flicking diamond droplets of water from his hair. He was about to move. And here she was, playing voyeur!

Belle stumbled to her feet and turned away. He'd looked so…elemental. An embodiment of masculine power that would both thrill and frighten any woman.

A sudden blast of need rocked her. Melting awareness. Choking heat. The desire to have those strong arms shelter her again. But this time his body would warm her in different ways and his hands would caress her.

She shook her head. This was absurd. She'd survived the ordeal of a lifetime: violence and pain, threat and terror. How could she even think about sexual attraction?

Had something fused in her brain? Or was this a primitive reaction to her near-fatal experience?

The urge to escape, to be alone with her confused emotions, was overwhelming. But there was nowhere to go. She was a prisoner here with her buccaneer.

Rafiq yanked the trousers up his wet legs and watched her stare out to sea, seeking some sign of rescue.

She looked lost and alone, her slender body held upright only by the steely determination he'd seen in her. Her hair was a matted nimbus around her head, not like the sleek style in her passport photo. Rings of bruised, bloody skin marked her ankles where the irons had bitten.

She should look pathetic, an object of sympathy, he told himself as he hauled his shirt on and strode towards her. Yet he saw only the streamlined perfection of her toned body. The inviting flare of her hips that had cradled him through the night till he'd thought he'd go mad, resisting urges that were nigh on irresistible. He read tensile strength in the set of her shoulders, in her wide-planted, honey-tanned legs.

He thrust aside the subtle voice of temptation.

'Ms Winters.' He saw her tense, but she didn't turn. 'How do you feel this morning?'

'Glad to be alive.' She half turned her head. 'And you?' There was strain in her profile, at odds with her determined chin and the strength of her neat, straight nose.

'All in one piece,' he responded, injecting a lightness into his tone that he didn't feel. 'We've had a lucky escape. Your colleague, Mr MacDonald, will be glad to see you.'

She nodded. Despite his better judgement, he allowed his gaze to slip down over her azure swimsuit. Her slim, perfect body dried his mouth. Sweat prickled his palms.

He wanted to erase the memory of last night—of her terror—in the simplest, most effective way. With pleasure. Carnal pleasure.

But eventually her rigid stillness penetrated his racing brain. Realisation hit and guilt flooded him.

No wonder she wouldn't turn to look at him! She was embarrassed, wearing a skintight swimsuit in front of a man she barely knew. That explained the high set of her shoulders, the tension humming through her every muscle.

She could only feel vulnerable after what she'd been through. Who knew what trauma she'd experienced?

A leaden weight settled in his belly as he thought of her, alone with a band of kidnapping thugs. He wanted to reach out and comfort her. But that would be a mistake.

As if to confirm it, she shifted, edging away.

'A rescue team will be on its way as soon as possible,' he assured her.

She nodded, but stood aloof. She looked as fragile as spun glass. It wouldn't take much to shatter her.

A ray of sunlight illuminated her golden hair and limned her sleekly curved body. Something caught at his breath, deep down in his chest. He frowned. He'd known more beautiful women. Had more beautiful women. Gorgeous, consciously seductive women. But Isabelle Winters stirred his blood in a way he'd never experienced.

Was it her incredible inner strength? Her bravery? Or the way she carried herself—like royalty—despite the barbarous manacles and her state of undress?

Or perhaps it was because she was the only woman he'd ever lain with all night and not made love to.

She swayed and he bit back an oath, registering her trembling knees and the stress lines that tightened her lips. Pain and reaction were finally taking their toll.

Rafiq grabbed her upper arms, tempering his hold to a gentle, sustaining pressure. He ignored the frisson of awareness that skimmed his palms at the contact, the skirl of heat that ignited in his gut.

Carefully, touching her as lightly as possible, he helped her to sit. Bending down close, he saw the pupils dilate in her wide blue eyes. She was in shock.

'You need to get warm.' Already he was unbuttoning his shirt. Her jaw was set as if against a chill, and her hands were clenched, white-knuckled together. He saw a tremor ripple right through her.

Her nipples pebbled against the thin blue fabric. And his lower body tightened in a telltale response that made him grit his teeth.

'I'm not cold,' she protested. 'We're in the tropics!'

'Nevertheless.' He dragged the shirt off his shoulders and draped it round her. She smelt warm and enticingly female. Awareness of her vulnerability tugged at his senses and he straightened, stepping away from her.

'You're hurt!' She'd seen his shoulder. Something had smashed into him last night and gashed him.

She raised her hands, pointing, and he sucked in his breath. She looked like a suppliant, kneeling at his feet. Ultra-feminine in his oversized shirt, breasts tilted up towards him by the movement of her arms.

She could have been some sexy modern-day slave, begging.

And in that instant, staring down at her, he felt a hot, primitive force surge in him. The instinct to reach out and grab. His blood quickened, his body hardened at the sensual image. At the idea of making her his. At the ruthless need to conquer and possess.

Generations of al Akhtar blood ran in his veins. Generations of fighters, leaders of men, pirates. His ancestors had been renowned for their rapacious passion and the single-minded pursuit of what they wanted.

Who could fight centuries of conditioning?

Already he could taste her sweetness like a drug on his tongue. Every muscle tensed like iron and his pulse drummed hard in anticipation. He remembered the feel of her beneath him, the combination of softness and strength, and knew she'd be perfect for him.

He only had to reach out. To take.

And then he registered her wide stare, the confusion in her eyes. Reality crashed upon him. He shook his head, trying to clear the miasma that fogged his brain.

'You're injured,' she said again.

'It's nothing.' His voice was brusque.

Her hands dropped to her knees, her clear bright gaze slid from his.

He was the worst kind of savage. Ill-tempered because compassion, the rules of civilised society, his sense of responsibility, all proclaimed she wasn't for him. He shouldn't want her. Not so elementally, so viscerally.

Yet it was so.

The first time he'd looked into her eyes sizzling fire had blasted through him. It scorched him still.

But he had an obligation to protect her.

'Let me see how badly you're hurt.' His voice was low, brushing across her sensitive nerves like the stroke of plush fur on bare skin. Belle darted a look up and found him still watching her.

Instead of dark eyes to match his black-as-night hair, his eyes were a deep, clear green. An exact match for the enticing crystal water where she'd dived this past week.

She stared, enthralled by a flicker of heat in those cool, sexy eyes.

Yet his face was hard, its strong lines set with disapproval. Had he guessed her secret thoughts? Recognised the delicious thrill that shivered through her as he towered over her? Or her rush of excitement as he'd stripped off his shirt to reveal that powerful, muscular chest?

It took all her will-power to keep her gaze fixed on his face, not follow the arrowing line of dark, masculine hair that invited her attention down his belly.

With his superb fitness, his air of supreme competence and control, he must belong to some élite rescue squad. The sort called in when things got really tough.

And with those looks he probably had adoring women throwing themselves at him with monotonous regularity.

No doubt he was hoping the wreck of a woman he'd just saved wouldn't follow suit.

Embarrassment heated her cheeks as she watched his mouth firm into a narrow line. He knew what she felt, all right, but he was gentleman enough to ignore her weakness. If she was lucky he'd dismiss it as a product of post-traumatic stress. As she intended to.

'Ms Winters.' In one supple move he sat before her and reached out one hand, palm up. 'Let me see your wrists.'

Wordlessly she complied, sucking in a long, calming breath as he took her hands in his and concentrated his attention on her torn, bruised skin. She already knew the touch of those long, capable fingers, the brush of calluses against her flesh. But familiarity didn't prevent the melting sensation that spread through her.

'It's Belle,' she said at last, her voice uneven.

'Belle.' He paused, her name on his tongue, and fire shot down to the centre of her being. He lifted his head to meet her eyes. 'And you must call me Rafiq.'

She nodded. 'Rafiq.' She should have guessed even his name would be sexy.

'Your hands are knocked about, but with antibiotics to ward off infection they should heal.' He opened his hands and she slid hers out of his hold.

'Let me see your ankles now.' He reached down and lifted her foot in one hand, gently brushing the sand away.

'Not too bad, considering,' he said finally, after a close inspection. 'If you're lucky you'll only have minimal scarring.'

Belle nodded, relieved when he released her. His nearness, even the whisper of his warm breath against her skin, set her senses reeling. She was so utterly attuned to him she was sure he could read the longing in her gaze.

'Do you have any other injuries?' Was that a thread of tension she detected in his tone?

She turned from her contemplation of the empty ocean to find his attention fixed on her thigh. A large, multicoloured bruise marred her leg—unmistakably the mark of a massive hand.

Belle shuddered as she remembered getting that bruise. Heavy, thickset men, rank with the smell of sour sweat and excitement. Cruel eyes that told her they'd enjoyed maiming Duncan, would enjoy hurting her. For an instant she was sucked back into the nightmare, confused and fighting the choking panic that threatened to take hold.

She blinked, forcing herself to put aside the memory. There were more sore spots round her waist. Tentatively she touched them and winced.

'A couple of bruises,' she said, aiming for a matter-of-fact tone and failing. 'They'll heal in time.'

A burst of guttural Arabic, savage and uncompromising, broke across her words. Startled, she raised her eyes to see a look of such fierce emotion on Rafiq's face that she flinched. It was as if he'd transformed into a stranger. An intense, deadly stranger.

Then his eyes met hers and the impression was dispelled, his face smoothing out into the familiar mask of cool control.

'Forgive me, Ms Winters—Belle.' He paused, and she noticed the rapid tic of his pulse at the base of his throat. Not so calm, then.

He gestured abruptly to the livid bruise on her leg. 'This is untenable. That my countrymen have treated you in this way—' He bit off the words and drew in a breath that made his broad chest heave. 'Apologies are insufficient for such a crime. But, for what it's worth, you have mine.'

She shook her head, bemused. 'It's not your fault, Rafiq. You rescued us. Put yourself in danger to help.'

A single slashing movement of his hand cut her off.

'It sickens me that you have suffered violence at the hands of these men. Abduction and harm. When you are on the mainland, have no fear, you will be given the best of medical service. Counselling—whatever is appropriate.'

She watched him stretch out his fingers in a deliberate movement of forced relaxation. It was totally at odds with the tension in his big frame.

'And while you recuperate your attackers will be brought to justice. They will not long escape their punishment.' The stormy light in his eyes sent a thrill of apprehension skittering down her spine.

He paused. 'We have extremely competent female doctors who can take care of you and discuss your…experiences.'

He turned his gaze from her as if to give her privacy. And in that moment she realised why he'd been so outraged at the sight of her injuries. Embarrassment warred with relief and the need to reassure him.

'Rafiq,' she said, reaching out to touch his hand before she could change her mind. His fingers curled round hers and a jolt of blazing energy shot through her.

'They didn't…' She hesitated. 'They only hurt me to get me to move, to obey them. They didn't…'

'Rape you?' His voice was a husky murmur.

'No.'

She was fine. Really. She'd survived. Her injuries were minor. So why did the recollection of her kidnappers' avid eyes upset her? Why did she choke on the bitter taste of tears that blocked her throat and prickled her eyes?

'*Habibti*,' Rafiq murmured, touching her cheek in a feather-light caress that loosened her hold on her welling emotions even further. 'You've been through so much. There's no need to fight yourself as well. There is no shame in feeling upset.'

She responded to the sound of his voice, rich and warm, as much as to his words. Blindly she nodded, instinctively leaning towards the comfort of his solid frame. His hands closed round her arms and her rigid control slipped another notch. She felt as if she were unravelling, the very core of her loosening, unwinding, fraying. The dam that held her emotions in check splintered. Relief and remembered terror roiled within her in great, sickening waves.

For a long moment he held her at a distance, his hands supportive, bracing. The first sob rose in her throat, raw and wretched. And with one decisive movement of superb strength he lifted her, pulling her into his arms to cradle her against his torso.

His lips moved against her hair, whispering words of reassurance as she cried out her pain. He rocked her slowly. The heat of his body seeped into the chill of hers and the scent of him, of sea and musk, banished the lingering taste of rancid horror from her mouth. His heart was steady beneath her ear, calming, powerful.

Finally the storm of grief and pain eased.

Belle felt herself float, boneless and weightless, in his embrace. She hiccoughed, and the tears eventually subsided, and still he held her, murmuring in that magnificent velvety voice that filled her senses.

She never wanted to move again. She could stay here for ever.

Then she heard it. The rhythmic thud in the distance. The swell of unmistakable sound as a helicopter approached. Safe in Rafiq's arms, she listened to the noise grow louder and closer, knowing it meant rescue but strangely feeling neither relief nor exhilaration.

Now the roar was directly overhead. Swirling sand bit into

her bare legs. She struggled to raise her heavy head, to pull herself out of Rafiq's arms. But he held her close.

'Shh, little one. No need to move yet.'

And it was easier to subside against him. She felt as if every ounce of strength she'd ever had, even the dogged determination that had kept her going through the last terrifying days, had drained away.

The chopper blades cut out into a silence that reverberated with their echo. Rafiq straightened against her, though still he held her close.

She should move. Reluctantly she lifted her head, peering through slitted, puffy eyes into the glare.

A group of men strode towards them from the huge helicopter. Two of them she recognised. Dawud, looking even more villainous than he had last night, with his burgeoning grey-flecked stubble and piercing dark eyes. And a younger man in pale trousers and a jacket. The British Consul to Q'aroum. She'd met him when she'd arrived.

There was no Australian Consul on the islands. But Duncan was British, and his government had supported the international marine expedition, eager for closer ties with the small oil-rich nation.

Dawud spoke rapidly in Arabic. She read urgency in his gestures, felt the answering tension in Rafiq's muscled frame. He barked out a query, and another, then was silent.

Finally David Gillham, the Consul, stepped forward. 'Your Highness, may I express—?'

'Highness?' Belle's interjection was muffled within Rafiq's embrace.

David Gillham paused, eyes serious. 'Ms Winters, you remember me?'

She nodded, struggling to sit upright in Rafiq's hold. His arms were like solid metal, binding her close.

'I remember you, Mr Gillham.' At last Rafiq's arms relaxed and she sat straighter. Immediately she wished she hadn't, feeling every man's gaze on her.

'It's good to see you again,' she said.

'And you, Ms Winters. It's a great relief to see you safe and sound.' His gaze slid from hers to Rafiq's.

'Er, it seems a little formality may be called for?' He watched her companion, as if seeking approval.

Rafiq nodded once, sharply.

David Gillham cleared his throat. 'Allow me to introduce you, Ms Winters, to Sheikh Rafiq Kamil Ibn Makram al Akhtar, Sovereign Prince of Q'aroum.'

CHAPTER THREE

RAFIQ nodded to the guard posted outside Belle's hospital room.

'Your Highness.' A doctor hurried forward. 'I'm afraid Ms Winters is sleeping now. You may wish to return later.'

'Then it will be a short visit,' Rafiq replied, moving forward as the guard opened the door.

He didn't pause to analyse this compulsion to see her.

All day he'd done his duty. Touring sites on the outer islands hit by the cyclone. Organising the deployment of resources for disaster relief. Meeting with the Cabinet and national security advisors to assess the political fall-out from the kidnappings and receive briefings on the search for those responsible. Each meeting, each need, more urgent than the last.

Now he did something purely for himself. Something he'd wanted to do ever since he'd relinquished Belle Winters into the charge of the medics on the helicopter. He breathed deeply and entered her room.

Shutters softened the late-afternoon light, reinforcing the quiet. Immediately his gaze fixed on the narrow, hospital regulation bed in the centre of one wall. Bright blonde hair framed a face that was far too pale. Her eyes were closed and she lay unmoving under the white cotton sheet.

Rafiq's heart thudded hard against his ribcage. Surely she

was too still? He couldn't discern any movement, not even her breathing.

He strode across the room as the doctor murmured from behind him, 'She's been asleep for hours, Highness. She may not wake until tomorrow. We can contact you when she does.'

Rafiq stopped at the bedside, hands clasped tight behind his back. It was a gesture he'd learned years ago from his grandfather. There were times when a man needed to take action. But a royal sheikh must always appear calm, unmoved.

So Rafiq schooled his expression as he stood looking down at her, skimming his gaze over the form that seemed so fragile, so unprotected, beneath the starched sheet. Finally he discerned the gentle rise of her chest as she inhaled, and the tension gripping him eased a fraction.

Of course she was alive. What had he thought? That the medical staff didn't know their jobs? Exhaustion, they'd said. Exposure and dehydration. But not severe enough to be life-threatening.

She'd been lucky.

Rafiq considered the bandages on her wrists, the blistered skin of her shoulders, the drip attached to her arm, the vulnerability of her slight form.

His hands clenched into tight fists as a surge of adrenaline flooded him. Hot fury twisted low in his belly as he contemplated the men who'd done this to her.

Lucky!

She was indeed lucky to be alive. Lucky her captors hadn't returned to the island for a little sport. Lucky they'd decided to let their victims die an ugly, lingering death from thirst rather than finish them off with a blade to the throat. Or worse.

Lucky the gang's ringleader hadn't taken part in the kidnapping personally. Selim al Murnah was a connoisseur of cruelty. A man who wouldn't miss an opportunity to indulge his sick whims on such a lovely woman.

The idea of Belle at Selim's mercy was revolting. The bitter taste of bile rose in Rafiq's throat as he recognised how narrowly she'd escaped death and torture.

His gaze roved her features, so familiar after such a short time. Her golden hair, her straight, determined nose, the sculpted, bone-deep beauty of her face. Her lips: cracked and dry, but undeniably seductive. A mouth created to please a man. A courtesan's mouth. A mouth that had tempted him, haunted him, since he'd first seen her in the glare of the torchlight—half naked, beyond exhausted, and heartbreakingly brave.

'Highness?' The murmured word made him start. He turned his head to meet the worried frown of the doctor.

'Very well.' Rafiq inclined his head. 'I see you're doing all you can for Ms Winters. Be assured of my gratitude. She and Mr MacDonald are important guests. Keep me informed of their progress.'

The doctor nodded. 'Of course, Highness.'

As Rafiq turned to leave something caught his eye. A tentative movement against the stark sheet. He looked across to see her brow pucker, her eyes slowly open. Something caught at his throat, restricting his breathing, as he watched recognition spark in her gaze, her eyes widen.

'You came,' she whispered, her voice a hoarse whisper. At the sound of it some of the stiffness across his neck and shoulders melted.

He reached down and took her hand in his, squeezing gently, as if he could transfer some of his strength to her. Her hand was slim, cool, frighteningly limp within his grasp.

'Of course I came, little one. You didn't think I'd abandon you?'

She didn't answer, just stared up at him from those mesmerising azure eyes. The impact of that look struck him in the solar plexus, sending a jolt of sizzling sensation through him. Then her eyelids flickered shut and her hand went lax in his.

'If I may, Highness?'

Reluctantly Rafiq relinquished Belle's hand to the doctor, and stepped back while he took her pulse.

'She's fine,' the doctor said after a moment, answering his unspoken question. 'Merely sleeping.' He paused. 'Perhaps she will rest better after seeing Your Highness? She seemed to take comfort from your presence.'

There was the faintest trace of speculation in his well-modulated tones. But Rafiq knew enough about his people and the power of speculation to be prepared.

'I was one of the team who found Mr MacDonald and Ms Winters,' he explained. 'I'd be surprised if they didn't recognise us.'

'As you say.' The doctor gestured for Rafiq to precede him out of the room. 'It would be remarkable indeed.'

Rafiq resisted the urge to turn, to look again at Belle. Instead he followed the doctor out into the corridor.

Duncan McDonald's room was identical to Belle's, but the shutters were open, letting in late-afternoon sun that lit his red hair to flame. His leg was in traction, his arm connected to a drip and his chest bandaged. He'd been injured while trying to protect Belle Winters from the abductors.

A brave man. So why was Rafiq reluctant to meet him?

He crossed the room and waited while the doctor performed the introductions.

'Mr MacDonald, it's gratifying to see you looking so much better.'

'Your Highness.' Duncan paused, as so many Westerners did over the title. 'I must thank you. I understand you were responsible for our rescue?'

'There's no need for thanks, Mr MacDonald. We are simply glad you and Ms Winters are now safe.'

'Belle! How is she?' There was no mistaking the desperate edge in the other man's voice.

'Ms Winters is sleeping. The doctor assures me she will recover completely.'

Duncan slumped back against the pillows and sighed. 'I feel responsible for her.'

Rafiq knew how he felt. At least MacDonald had the solace of knowing he'd done his best to protect her. It was for Rafiq to feel the full weight of guilt, since he was the ultimate cause of their danger. That realisation was like a canker, eating at his peace.

'On behalf of all Q'aroumis, may I express our deep regret at this terrible incident? Our security forces are scouring the country even now in search of your kidnappers.'

'They'll be tried?'

'Of course.' Rafiq's smile was grim. 'We no longer administer rough justice in Q'aroum. You can look forward to testifying at the legal proceedings against them.'

Duncan MacDonald nodded. 'If you catch them.'

'Oh, they'll be caught.' He'd see to it personally. Selim and his followers would be hunted down like rabid dogs. They wouldn't escape justice after what they'd done.

Rafiq stifled the urge to pace. Political dissent was one thing. But violent plots couldn't be tolerated. The kidnapping was part of Selim's wider scheme to destabilise Q'aroum's democratic system. He hid behind extremist ideology but sought only personal power.

'If you hadn't turned up when you did—' Duncan MacDonald began, but Rafiq cut him off with an impatient gesture. He didn't want MacDonald's thanks.

'You'd have survived. I'm sure Ms Winters would have seen to it. She's a remarkable woman.'

Yet he knew how close the search had come to missing that one small atoll. Just as well he'd insisted on taking a personal role in the operation. His inside knowledge of Selim, his second cousin, had helped concentrate the search in the right area. If it hadn't been for that…

'Tell me,' he said, focussing again on the man before him. 'Is there anything we can do to make your stay more comfortable?'

'Well, there is one thing.' Duncan MacDonald hesitated. 'My girlfriend doesn't have a visa for Q'aroum, and I know they take weeks to process.'

Rafiq felt his facial muscles stretch wide as he smiled. His first genuine smile since this business began. So MacDonald had a girlfriend back home in Britain.

'I'll have it organised immediately.' He paused, as if considering. 'We must ask Ms Winters when she wakes whether she has a similar request.'

Duncan MacDonald shook his head. 'No need. Belle doesn't have a boyfriend waiting at home for her.'

Ah. Now, that was interesting.

Belle sank back gratefully against the limousine's soft leather seat. At last she was on her way.

After three days in hospital she'd been climbing the walls with impatience. But the medical staff had been insistent: she mustn't leave until they were sure there were no complications, until she'd recovered her strength. Anyone would think they'd had orders to keep her immured there. It had only been when she'd threatened to leave without a formal discharge that the doctor had agreed to release her.

And now this. She surveyed the sumptuous interior of the vehicle with a frown. Surely an ordinary taxi would have done? She wasn't a VIP.

She stared out of the window as the engine purred into life

and they swept out of the hospital forecourt. She should be excited at the prospect of returning to her lodgings. Of resuming work again. After all, she'd made marine archaeology the centre of her life for years now—was just starting to build a modest reputation as an up-and-coming researcher in her field.

There was so much to catch up on. She'd call the maritime archaeology centre and discuss a replacement for Duncan. And she'd better check the wreck site to see if the cyclone had damaged the ship or covered it again. It had been in remarkable condition for a vessel that had been underwater for two millennia. She couldn't bear the thought of it being destroyed just as they found it.

And tonight she'd make another long call home, to reassure her mum. Then a hot, soothing bath. Bliss!

She shifted on the padded seat. Why wasn't she more excited to be on her way? There was a niggle of tension in the pit of her stomach that she'd tried to ignore ever since she'd left her hospital room. A niggle that had grown alarmingly into a tight, hard knot of fear.

Fear that alone in the expedition team's house she might not be safe. That masked men might burst in, brandishing guns.

She'd relived the nightmare of abduction so often that she could barely believe it was over. *Surely* it was over? The doctor had spoken of political strife, had implied she and Duncan had been merely in the wrong place at the wrong time. Yet still the anxiety lingered.

Belle wondered if she'd ever lose it.

She stared out at the brightly lit streets, finding some comfort in the quaint and vibrant old city. They passed a huge square where the colourful night markets were in full swing. She loved the medieval town, with its maze of streets and its unexpected open spaces.

The car took a sharp corner and Belle looked up to see the

palace, illuminated like a fairytale castle. It reminded her of long-buried fantasies. Of Arabian nights and genies and magic carpets. On two sides, facing the sea, it was a brooding fortress, its centuries-old walls a solid bastion against invaders' cannon. But from this side the royal buildings were an Arabian fantasy: gardens and fountains, pavilions, gilt domes, arches, and screens adorned with delicate carved tracery.

'Hey, you can't go in here!' Belle scooted forward on her seat as the car turned into the private palace road.

The driver ignored her, pulling to a halt at the ornate iron gates barring their way. A man in uniform stepped out of the shadows and spoke briefly to the chauffeur. Then, to Belle's amazement, he waved them on as the gates slid open.

'What are you doing?' Her voice was husky with disbelief. 'This isn't where I'm going.'

The driver's voice was calm. 'I was told to bring you here, ma'am. There's no mistake.'

She sank back in her seat, her heart thudding as the car proceeded towards the palace. As the lights grew closer, and her pulse raced faster, Belle forced herself to face the only logical explanation: she'd been brought here to meet him. The man she'd known as Rafiq. Who had turned out to be a royal prince, ruler of Q'aroum.

The man she'd spent the last few days trying to forget.

The man who'd seen her at her weakest, who'd recognised her despair and comforted her with his body and his soothing words. Who knew her vulnerability and her needs almost better than she did. Who'd read the raw, physical hunger in her eyes when she'd looked at him and had been repelled by it.

She swallowed. Did she have any hope of avoiding this interview?

Of course she didn't.

The car slid to a halt and a man in long pale robes came

forward to open the door for her. Quickly she smoothed her hair, ignoring the fine tremor in her hands. She was hardly dressed for a royal interview—but then, what was new? At least this time she *was* dressed. She tilted her chin up, hoping bravado would overcome embarrassment.

Rafiq al Akhtar had saved her life, and she owed him her thanks. It would be humiliating, facing him, reading the knowledge in his eyes, but it would soon be over. And then she'd never have to see him again.

'*Masa'a alkair*, Ms Winters. Good evening. You are welcome.' It was Dawud, the man who'd brought Duncan back to safety. He looked different, in flowing robes and a turban. She wondered if he wore his knife concealed beneath the swathed cotton.

'*Masa'a alkair*, Dawud.'

He smiled at her, a twist of the lips that tugged at his scar, and her tension eased fractionally.

'It's good to see you, Dawud.'

'And you, Miss Winters. Please, this way.' He gestured to the huge bossed wooden doors and ushered her inside. A pair of servants stood silent just inside the foyer.

As she accompanied him across the wide marble floor, the enormous double doors closed with a reverberating thud behind them. The sound made her falter. It was like the slam of a cell door: final and forbidding.

Belle straightened her shoulders, cursing her over-active imagination. She was no prisoner. This would be a short, formal audience. Nothing to panic about.

They crossed a reception room the size of an auditorium. Thank goodness Rafiq hadn't decided to see her here, where the elaborate raised dais with its gilt canopy would reinforce the power and pomp of his royal status. She already dreaded this interview. She didn't need a reminder of the yawning chasm between them.

Eventually Dawud knocked on a pair of carved doors.

'Come.'

The hair stood up on the back of Belle's neck as she recognised Rafiq's voice. It had haunted her dreams for three days. Sometimes its honeyed tones had lulled her with the lyrical, comforting flow of foreign words. But just as often that voice had thrilled her with its deep, masculine promise, till she woke edgy and aroused, unable to sleep again for the knowledge of her own desperate weakness.

How much of it had been her imagination? Surely no man, no matter how handsome, could affect her so elementally?

Dawud stood, holding the door open for her, and she took a deep breath, knowing that the reality of this meeting couldn't be as bad as she feared. She stepped through the door and stalled in her tracks.

Belle knew she was staring. Knew she should say something, anything. But her tongue stuck to the roof of her mouth. She wiped clammy hands down her cotton trousers and realised she'd been completely, devastatingly wrong.

Her imagination hadn't exaggerated. Rafiq was everything she'd thought him. And more.

'Belle. Please, come in.' He walked towards her, closing in on her personal space, till she felt cocooned by his aura, surrounded by his energy. Yet he stopped several paces from her, his sea-green gaze impenetrable. His austere face compelling.

He was as tall as she remembered, as broad across the shoulders. His hair was tied back, slick as if wet from a recent shower, and he wore a long robe of fine cotton, grey shot through with misty green. It reminded her of foggy seas and hidden secrets. In contrast, the vertical slash down from the robe's neckline revealed a few inches of hard, tanned, uncompromising male.

She drew a faltering breath and forced herself to meet his

gaze. She thrust away the seductive memory of him, water sluicing off his smooth, bare flesh, as he emerged from the sea.

'Your Highness—'

'No! Rafiq, please.' He reached out and took her hand in his, his warmth enveloping her as he tugged her further into the room, closer to him.

'Rafiq,' she said, then stopped, breathless, as he smiled at her. Emerald lights shimmered in his eyes, and the curve of his lips transformed his face from sombre to breathtaking.

Her heart thumped hard against her ribs and her mouth tilted up in automatic response. The feel of his large hand encompassing hers triggered memories of his hard, muscled body pressed intimately against her, protecting her all through that long night. Heat flared in her cheeks.

'It's good to see you looking so well.' His words were a low caress that mesmerised her and brought her skin to tingling life.

Over her shoulder, Dawud's voice pierced the charged atmosphere. 'Ms Winters has just been released from hospital. She must be weary.'

'Of course. I won't keep her late.' Rafiq's dark eyebrows drew together in a straight line as he looked past her, clearly annoyed at the interruption. 'You may leave us now.' His tone was brusque.

'Goodnight, Ms Winters,' Dawud said from the doorway.

'Goodnight, Dawud.' Belle turned, trying and failing to ignore the fact that Rafiq still held her hand in his. 'Thank you for all you did for us. For me and Duncan.'

Dawud bowed. 'There is no need for thanks, Ms Winters.' And then he was gone, silently closing the doors.

'Come.' Rafiq drew her with him and led her across the room. Heat throbbed up her arm from his touch and spread right through her. She inhaled his scent: warm, spicy and male. Something quivered into life deep within her. A response, a thrill that was purely instinctive.

'Here.' He gestured to a low sofa, covered with plump embroidered cushions. 'Please make yourself comfortable.'

When she sat he sank down onto another sofa opposite her. But even with that distance between them Belle recognised the tug of awareness, the shimmer of desire pulsing through her body, heating her skin. It was unnerving, this vibrant, palpable connection between them. She'd never felt anything like it.

Perhaps the hospital staff had been right and she needed more rest. Surely this potent reaction wasn't normal?

'How are you feeling?' he asked.

'As good as new,' she said immediately. 'They were wonderful in the hospital. Really terrific.' And now she was babbling. Great.

'The medical staff expected you to stay longer.' His gaze was intent.

'You talked to them?'

He nodded. 'We were all very concerned for you and your colleague, Mr MacDonald.'

Of course. It would have been embarrassing for the Q'aroumi government if she or Duncan had died. There'd been no personal interest in Rafiq's enquiries. Why should there be? She was just a troublesome foreigner. Yet, beyond all logic, it still rankled that he hadn't visited her in the hospital. She'd lain there for days thinking of him, dreaming of him, waiting for him to stride into her room.

And as her disappointment had grown, so had her awareness of her own folly. Did she really expect a royal visit to her bedside? That was laughable. Especially in a country where the Prince wasn't a figurehead but an active head of state, busy with the affairs of government.

She pulled herself together.

'I have to thank you,' she said, plastering a bright smile on her face and looking straight into his eyes. She shivered at the illusion of heat she saw there, and at the tell-tale tightness in her chest. But she ignored both and plunged on. 'Without your inter-vention Duncan and I would have died. We owe you our lives.'

'You owe me nothing, Belle. You were an innocent victim. It was my duty to find you.' He paused. 'Just as it's my duty now to keep you safe.'

She frowned. 'But I *am* safe.'

Surely she was? The kidnappers could have no further interest in her. Yet suddenly dread caught the breath in her lungs, clamped down on her shoulders. The memory of leering masked faces swam before her eyes. The thought of her isolated lodgings sent a cold shiver through her.

'I will make sure you are.' Rafiq's voice was deep, as if making a pledge. His expression was steely, his jaw tight.

'We will take no chances with your well-being. Until the man-hunt is over you will reside here. In the palace.'

CHAPTER FOUR

STAY in the palace? Here? Where he lived? Where she'd see him and be taunted by the impossible fantasies she just couldn't prevent when he was near? No, thanks.

'That's not necessary.' Belle was pleased she sounded so calm, so reasonable, despite her suddenly frenetic heartbeat and the frisson of appalled excitement skittering up her spine.

'It is necessary, and so it will be.' His tone was implacable, his expression determined.

Belle raised a hand to her brow, frowning. She felt as if she'd walked into an alternative reality. One where the unthinkable happened. But after the events of the last days anything seemed possible.

'Are you in pain?' There was concern in his voice, belying the relaxed poise of his body.

Slowly she shook her head. 'I'm fine. Just confused.' And tired. Suddenly so very, very tired.

'You need rest. We can discuss this in the morning.'

'No!'

He raised his brows, every inch the supercilious monarch. For the first time she saw in him the bone-deep arrogance of a man born and bred to rule.

'I'd rather discuss it now,' she said. 'Surely there's no danger any more to me or Duncan?' But even as she said it she remembered the armed guards posted in the hospital corridors. The thought made her stomach muscles cramp convulsively. Anxiety was never far away now.

'Don't fret, Belle. You are safe here. Nothing will harm you. You have my word on it.' Absolute assurance deepened his voice and glinted in his eyes, and Belle responded automatically to his certainty. She felt the tension in her ease a fraction as she met his gaze.

It was inexplicable, but from the first moment she'd seen Rafiq, that night on her prison island, she'd instinctively trusted in his ability to protect her. Even against the force of nature.

'But I will take no chances,' he continued. 'Those behind your kidnapping are desperate. And desperate men act rashly. Especially since they were thwarted of their original purpose. I will keep you close, where I can be sure of your safety.'

She shook her head. The idea of Rafiq keeping her close conjured up far too many insane ideas. Fantasies she'd promised herself not to think of again.

And his reasoning escaped her. She'd gleaned from the hospital staff that the kidnapping had been some political gesture, designed to stir an international incident. No one wanted to harm her now. It wasn't as if they had a personal grudge against her. Her mind felt thick, her thought processes dull, as she tried to follow his argument.

'I'd rather return to the team's house.' She had to get back to her safe routine, where she could immerse herself in work and try to forget what had happened. Especially now she'd discovered her weakness for Rafiq hadn't been imaginary—part of the surreal experiences of the past few days.

This attraction was all too real. It was there in her nervous pulse, her uneven breathing, the effervescence in her blood. She'd experienced nothing like it before, and that scared her.

'I'll be fine there, and quite safe. No one will bother me.'
Was it Rafiq she was trying to convince, or herself?

'You will stay here.' His tone brooked no argument, just as
if she had no say in the matter. The look in his eyes told her he
had no intention of being swayed by anything as trifling as her
preferences.

She felt her hackles rise. 'I think that's ultimately my
decision,' she snapped, then caught her lip between her teeth
as she watched his brows furrow into a black scowl. However
unreasonable, he was her host—and a royal prince.

'While you're in Q'aroum I am responsible for your safety.'
He spoke patiently, as if explaining the obvious. 'For such time
as I permit your expedition in our waters.'

Belle's breath snagged at the audacity of the man. Had he just
threatened her, ever so subtly? Reminded her that her presence
here, and that of the expedition, rested on his goodwill?

His scowl disappeared, and now his face was unreadable.
His eyes gave nothing away, but he watched her with an unnerving intensity that made her breath catch.

Surely she was imagining things. He wouldn't threaten the
future of the expedition if she refused to stay in the palace.
Would he? No, that would be ludicrous.

'Come.' Abruptly he stood, and held out his hand. 'We'll
discuss this later, and I'll explain in as much detail as you
require. In the meantime you need rest.'

Ridiculous to feel so weak after days in bed, but her head
swam as she stood up. His hand, warm and strong at her elbow,
held her steady and she was grateful for his support.
Nevertheless, she refused to be railroaded into such an arrangement. She tilted her chin up and met his eyes. 'Thank you for
your kind offer, Your Highness—'

'But you want to argue about it?' There was a glimmer of
something that might have been humour in his cool eyes as he

slid his hand down to hers. 'Never mind. We can debate it all you wish in the morning.'

He smiled then, and she stared, dazzled by the instant transformation in him. From scowling autocrat to sexy, mesmerising flesh-and-blood man simply with a curve of his lips. And his eyes: they smiled down at her as if inviting her to enjoy some intimate shared jest. His thumb stroked across her hand in a gesture that sent ripples of longing through her. She felt herself sway towards him, and prayed it was fatigue that made her unsteady on her feet.

'Ms Winters,' he said at last, his voice low and coaxing, his eyes hooded. 'Would you do me the honour of staying as my guest here tonight? It would be some small recompense for the ordeal you've been through to let us offer you some true Q'aroumi hospitality.'

When he put it like that…

'I…' Her voice was a hoarse croak. Did this man have any idea of the sheer sexual appeal he generated when he put his mind to it?

'That would be very pleasant,' she said at last in a choked voice. She'd been outmanoeuvred and there wasn't a thing she could do about it. 'Thank you for the invitation.'

'Good.' His strong fingers closed tight around hers, generating a flare of heat that burned right through her defences. She stared into his eyes and felt herself falling, like a diver entering unknown waters.

'And in the morning,' he said with a satisfied smile, 'we will discuss the rest of your stay.'

The sun was high in the sky when Belle woke in the wide, low, luxurious bed. She listened to the cascading notes of an unfamiliar songbird somewhere outside, watched the filtered light play across the delicate wall paintings of fruit and flowers.

She was alive. She was safe.

She was in Rafiq's home.

The realisation brought her instantly awake as fleeting snatches of her dreams swirled in her mind. They'd been dominated yet again by a tall, fatally attractive pirate. An arrogant prince who'd demanded she obey his every command.

She squirmed as she recalled how intimate some of those commands had been, and how eagerly her dream self had complied. How she'd revelled in his dominance. She, who'd never let any man control her!

Abruptly she flung off the light silk coverlet and swung her legs out of bed.

She should be thankful her subconscious mind had focussed on something other than the mind-numbing terror that had haunted her for days. Amazingly, terror hadn't stalked her sleep. Yet the alternative—taunting, erotic dreams featuring Rafiq as her lover—was untenable.

She'd lived a nun-like existence for the past couple of years—every waking hour committed to her work, much of the time on location in isolated areas with no time for socialising, for romance. Maybe the dreams were the natural reaction of a young, healthy body to prolonged sexual abstinence.

She shook her head. Abstinence was something she'd learned to live with, especially after two short-lived attempts at what she'd hoped might become serious relationships. Men just weren't attracted by her absorption in her work, her travel or her independent mindset. She'd come to accept that romance would never figure prominently in her life. Or sex.

So what was happening to her? How did she explain the way she'd responded last night to Rafiq's smile? To the touch of his hand on hers? She'd felt as if the cyclone they'd weathered together had somehow lodged inside her, found its epicentre deep in the hidden feminine core of her, pulverising her defences and her inhibitions.

Belle shook her head. Last night she'd been exhausted. And she was vulnerable after all she'd endured, off-balance after her terrifying ordeal. The counsellor had warned her she wouldn't feel the full effects of the trauma straight away.

That was why she'd felt so strange—so fragile, yet so responsive. Post-traumatic stress. That had to be it. Her weakness last night had nothing to do with sea-deep eyes. With a voice like seductive velvet that could charm the birds from the trees. Or with the sheer physical presence of a man who was so much more than any man she'd ever met.

Today she'd prove it. She'd see Rafiq and she'd feel nothing but gratitude. And pleasure at the chance he'd given her to experience the luxury of a real palace.

Simple.

Thirty minutes later she followed a maid through a maze of corridors and out into a small courtyard.

Belle stopped, entranced. On all four sides the slender pillars of the colonnade supported high arches of intricate filigree work, carved from solid marble. A shallow pool filled the centre of the courtyard, surrounded by dozens of water jets and glossy citrus trees. The whisper of fountains and the scent of orange blossom filled the air, a seductive assault on the senses.

But it was the intricate mosaic on the base of the pool that snared her attention, richly hued and dazzlingly bright in the morning sun. It portrayed an enormous peacock, several metres long, its tail open in a stunning display that seemed to move in the rippling water.

The colours were brilliant, vibrant and glistening. But, more than that, the detailed artistry of the work was awe-inspiring. Belle moved to the edge of the tiled walkway, leaning closer for a better view.

'You like our peacock?' asked a low, sultry voice from the shadows.

Belle didn't need to look across the courtyard to know who spoke. She'd recognise that voice anywhere. Already her pulse quickened in anticipation. Feminine awareness was a tight coil circling in her belly. So much for her reaction last night being due to exhaustion. She was in trouble when just the sound of his deep voice did this to her!

She kept her eyes on the mosaic. 'It's spectacular. I've never seen anything like it.'

'The art of mosaic-making is highly prized in Q'aroum. You'll find small mosaics in many homes.' Rafiq's voice came nearer as he walked along the colonnade towards her. She clenched her hands tight, willing herself not to retreat.

'But you're right,' he said. 'You won't see another like this.' He stopped at her side. She could tell by the way her skin prickled, by the heat that blossomed in her breast and rose up to flush her neck and face.

And still she couldn't look at him. Didn't dare.

'See the way the sun catches and reflects the colours as if they held an inner fire?'

She nodded. 'The background—is that gilt work?'

'Close,' he murmured, and she knew by the puff of his warm breath on her hair that he'd turned to watch her. 'It's not gilt. It's solid gold.'

'What?' She swung her head to look at him, straight into his hard, handsome face. 'But there are square metres of the stuff!'

He shrugged. 'Ostentatious, I agree. But effective.' He looked down into her eyes and smiled, and her heart tumbled over.

'What else could do justice to the rest of it?' he added. 'The peacock itself is made of semi-precious stones. The purple is amethyst. The green is malachite and jade. There's amber and garnet, topaz and lapis-lazuli.'

Belle stared, unable to wrench her gaze from that smile, from those fathoms-deep green eyes.

'It must have cost a fortune.'

His rich chuckle echoed across the marble walls and she bit her lip, feeling gauche. What did it matter if it had cost a fortune? The Sheikhs of Q'aroum were fabled for their wealth.

'My ancestors had a taste for riches and loved to flaunt their possessions. This mosaic is several hundred years old, probably the result of a particularly successful season.'

'Season?' Belle asked, her brow knitting in bewilderment.

His smile widened into a grin that drew the stiffening out of her spine, leaving her weak, her knees like jelly.

'Buccaneering,' he explained, stepping closer so that she had to tilt her face up to watch him. 'For generations the Q'aroumis were pirates—extorting payment for safe passage through the Arabian Sea and, when it wasn't paid, plundering whatever they wanted.'

Belle sucked in a breath at the intensity of his raking gaze. The slanting rays of sunshine illuminated the hard angles of his face, highlighted the arrogant cast of his high cheekbones and aristocratic nose, caught the glitter of gold at his ear. A sizzle of primitive excitement trembled through her. Excitement and trepidation.

Once before she'd pictured him as a pirate, a man who'd reach out and grasp whatever he wanted whatever the cost or the danger. Now she saw that determination, that drive to possess, right here before her eyes. She had no trouble picturing him at the helm of a swift-sailing tall ship, plundering the sea lanes of whatever took his fancy.

Perhaps his barbaric inheritance was latent, close to the surface even in this modern-day monarch, who ruled a progressive nation funded by offshore oil revenues.

Belle swallowed hard, mesmerised by the glitter in Rafiq's

eyes, suddenly aware of the musky, enticing scent of his bronzed skin so close to hers.

'So, they grew rich on their plunder?' she said at last, her voice a mere whisper. She should have guessed. But she'd been so wrapped up in the ancient past she hadn't taken the time to learn the islands' more recent history. She'd known there'd been pirates in Q'aroum, but not that they'd been led by the royal family!

He nodded. 'And, as you can see, they enjoyed their wealth. The peacock is something of a family symbol.' He reached out and took her elbow in his hand, turning her to walk with him around the colonnade.

Belle concentrated on matching his steps, on keeping her breathing under control, not snatching desperate breaths in an effort to fill her suddenly empty lungs. Heat radiated out from his touch, searing her through the fabric of her shirt. Just like in last night's dreams, where their shared heat had been combustible.

'The bird is beautiful,' she said, desperate for conversation to cover her weakness. 'But it seems an unusual emblem.' Or, more precisely, an unusual emblem for a family that produced men like Rafiq. There was nothing gaudy or soft about him. He was all desert heat and masculine strength. And sheer sensual power.

He paused and gestured for her to precede him, to take a seat at a table set in the shade of the colonnade. She subsided gratefully onto a chair and looked away, out over the courtyard.

'It's one of two motifs you'll find throughout the palace,' he said, settling in a second chair. 'There's the falcon, prized for its speed and power, its prowess as a hunter. In less civilised times it was seen to represent all that was best in the men of my family. And then the peacock, symbol of the rich beauty of their wives. This part of the palace was designed as the harem— hence the mosaic, as a compliment to the Sheikh's women.'

Belle's eyes widened. A strange thrill skittered down her

back at the knowledge she'd actually spent the night in a sheikh's harem. In *his* harem.

Damn, she had it bad.

Two maids arrived, carrying pastries, a fruit platter and coffee. Rafiq nodded for them to put the food on the table, but his attention remained focussed on Belle.

She was a problem, and not only because of the political complications her presence created. She was at the centre of a conundrum that threatened the very future of his country. A conundrum to which he must find a solution. And yet it wasn't her significance in this constitutional minefield that had kept him awake and pondering long into the night. It was the woman herself: capable, feisty. Desirable.

'Please, help yourself,' he said, gesturing to the laden table between them.

She'd trembled when he'd taken her arm just now, swayed as if unsteady on her feet, and her apparent weakness disturbed him. Especially since he'd experienced her personal brand of stoic endurance on that deserted island.

Perhaps he should send for a doctor.

He scrutinised her flushed face, noting the way her gaze slid away to the table, as if unwilling to meet his eyes. Her breasts rose with her rapid, shallow breathing, snagging his attention, distracting him.

Perhaps it wasn't a doctor she needed.

He remembered the way she'd looked at him last night, as if she'd seen only him and nothing at all of her luxurious surroundings. The way she'd jumped at his touch, her pulse quickening.

Something—satisfaction—stirred inside him.

Perhaps she wasn't ill at all.

He poured coffee, strong and aromatic, for them both, then offered her milk, consciously tamping down on his urgent curiosity.

'Of course, it wasn't just gold and gems that my ancestors took as their right,' he said as he leaned back in his chair, surveying her.

'It wasn't?' She darted a look at him, then concentrated on the array of food before her.

'No,' he said slowly. 'They appropriated money, of course, and weapons and ships. But the al Akhtars have always had a taste for the best in all things.'

Rafiq watched her choose a pastry. The sun lit her shoulder-length honey-blonde hair with pure gold. Her eyes were as bright as any sapphire in the royal jewels. And those lips...

Suddenly, overwhelmingly, he wanted to feel those lips on him, cool and soft against his burning flesh.

'They had an eye for beauty in all its forms,' he said, his voice deepening of its own accord as he watched her. 'And their taste in women was renowned.'

She swallowed hard, half choking on a mouthful of sweet pastry.

'They weren't averse to snatching a beautiful woman off a ship bound for another port. They saw it as their right.' He leaned towards her over the table, ostensibly to select some fruit for his plate. This close, he read fascination mixed with outrage in her eyes. Fiery blue accusation blazed at him.

'Kidnapping as well as piracy, then! No wonder your family had a reputation for ruthlessness.'

He nodded. 'Of course by today's standards it would be barbaric. But only a couple of generations ago it was another matter. And it wasn't always as dire as you think. My great-grandmother had no wish to leave here after she'd been...liberated from a ship.'

Her eyes grew huge. 'Your own great-grandmother?' She shook her head in amazement.

Rafiq sat back, watching the play of emotions across her

face. 'She was more than happy to stay after she met my great-grandfather. She'd been on her way from England to India to marry some military man she hardly knew. Family lore has it that she and my great-grandfather made a love match of it.'

'But she couldn't have—'

'What?' He frowned. 'She couldn't have loved a man of my culture?' Pride sharpened his voice. Pride bred through hundreds of years of al Akhtar blood. Of absolute rule and unquestioned authority.

'No, no, not that.' She shook her head, and hair like spun gold flared round her. 'But how could she have accepted it? Become just one of many women in a harem?' There was genuine distress in her tight lips and her worried brow.

'Ah.' He sipped his coffee and sat back, strangely satisfied at her reaction. 'Your concern isn't for the cultural and racial divide between them, it is for her place in his affections. You are a romantic, Belle.'

She met his gaze steadily, her chin jutting in a gesture he recognised as characteristic. 'It seems hard that she should have had no choice in the matter. That she should have given up everything for him and he gave up nothing,' she said. 'Just took what he wanted.'

'What you say would be true—if she hadn't wanted him just as much.'

He watched her eyes widen, her lips part in surprise. She clearly hadn't considered the possibility that his ancestress had got exactly what she desired, however unorthodox her meeting with her future husband.

'Don't let it worry you, Belle.' He leaned forward and closed his hand over hers. Her hand was smaller than his, seemingly fragile, but strong and capable. Just like the woman herself.

'I told you it was a love match. They were faithful to each

other. He was young when he stole her away, and the harem was filled with his female relatives, not his wives.'

He slid his thumb over the sensitive skin of her palm and felt her shiver in response. It pleased him, intrigued him, that she reacted so readily to his touch. The pulse at the base of her neck was an agitated tattoo, revealing what she would no doubt rather hide. Her scent, fresh and inviting, rose to entice him.

'In fact,' he murmured, spurred on by some teasing inner demon as he leaned closer, 'the pair of them started a family tradition. Since that time the al Akhtar men have only ever taken one wife. And once they find their woman they never let her go.'

Her indrawn breath was loud in the silence. The instant tension between them so strong, so intimate, that he felt it in every taut muscle, saw it reflected in her stunned expression.

Abruptly he released her.

She slid her hands off the table, out of sight. But his fingers still felt the silken delicacy of her skin against his.

They itched to feel more.

She was a woman of contrasts. Determination and physical courage in such an alluring, feminine body. So brave, yet obviously scared by her response to him. He'd made himself her protector, yet she intrigued him as no other woman had.

She was right to be nervous.

He took a strawberry and bit into its lush fullness, enjoying the fresh tartness overlying its sweetness. But his eyes were on Belle as he ate. Would she be sweet as summer berries? Ripe and rewarding and luscious?

She avoided his gaze as she reached for her coffee.

'But now we need to discuss the present,' he said, watching her take a sip of the hot brew.

She tilted her head in acknowledgement.

'You said last night that you want to return to your team's lodgings.'

'That's right.' She nodded so emphatically that her hair swirled around her shoulders. 'I've got lots to organise. There'll be a replacement for Duncan arriving some time, and then the rest of the group. And I want to visit the wreck again as soon as possible.'

'It will not be as simple as that.' He lifted his own cup and swallowed some of the strong coffee.

She put her cup down and squared her shoulders, as if bracing for bad news. 'What's wrong? Is it the wreck? Has it been destroyed by the cyclone?'

He shook his head. In all the mopping-up operations after the devastation wreaked on the outer islands, checking an ancient wreck had not been a priority. 'No one has been to investigate. Our problem has nothing to do with your marine survey. It has to do with the ransom that was paid to save you.'

Her brows pleated in confusion. 'But you rescued us. Why would a ransom be paid?'

Clearly she hadn't caught up with the news from her hospital bed. Which meant the staff there had been remarkably discreet.

'There was reason to suppose you would come to harm if the ransom wasn't paid. Serious harm.' He frowned, remembering his advisors arguing over what action to take in response to the kidnap. As if there could have been any doubt once he'd realised the situation's gravity. 'Regrettably, the deadline for payment of the ransom came before we could get news to the mainland that you'd been found.'

'So,' she said slowly, 'the ransom was paid anyway?'

'That's right.'

'How much do we owe you?'

Rafiq stared, not believing his ears.

'How much was the ransom?' she asked again, just as if she meant to find the money somehow, and pay him back whatever the cost of her rescue.

'You misunderstand,' he said abruptly. His neck stiffened at the implication that he sought recompense for doing his duty and he clamped his jaw tight shut. He took a slow, calming breath. 'The ransom wasn't money. It was the Peacock's Eye.'

Her brows knit together. 'I've heard of that,' she said slowly. 'It's jewellery, isn't it?'

He nodded. The Eye was jewellery just as the Taj Mahal was a tombstone.

Belle Winters obviously wasn't like most visitors, who believed a trip to Q'aroum wasn't complete without a visit to see the royal gems. The Eye was the centrepiece of the collection: a dazzling necklace, ancient and heavy with the weight of solid gold and gems, designed to mimic the pattern on a peacock's tail feather. Its value was in its magnificent wealth: the huge emeralds alone were beyond price. But much more important was its historic and cultural significance to Q'aroum.

'It's jewellery,' Rafiq agreed wryly. 'But, more than that, it's an heirloom that holds unique significance in our heritage. For generations it's been the traditional gift of the royal Sheikh to his bride.'

Her jaw dropped.

'According to the custom of my people,' he continued, 'since I relinquished it in return for you, I've paid it as a bride price. Which means that, as far as Q'aroum is concerned, Belle, you are my affianced bride.'

CHAPTER FIVE

BRIDE. Affianced bride. Belle gaped as the words tumbled through her brain.

She'd recognised the glint of amusement in his eyes as he'd spoken of his ancestors and their rapacious habits. But he wasn't laughing now. The long grooves that bracketed his mouth were etched deep, the sharp angles of his cheekbones and his jaw were prominent, as if tension tightened his muscles.

Her stomach dipped on a rollercoaster of reaction.

Bride! To this man? It was impossible. Ludicrous.

And yet still he didn't smile.

An icy finger of foreboding slid down her spine, making her shiver.

Bride to this man. Out of nowhere flashed an image of her and Rafiq together. Close. Intimate. Heat flared in her cheeks, and surreptitiously she wiped her damp hands over her trousers.

Rafiq threatened her self possession, but not because he was a royal prince, head of state and a billionaire. It was Rafiq the man of elemental power, unstudied sex appeal and restrained passion who unsettled her. Scared her.

He'd already stalked her dreams and taken up residence in her subconscious. Now he was talking about her *life*.

'They think we're engaged?' Her voice cracked on the word.

'It is the custom.' He nodded, sounding appallingly calm. 'Though of course usually the Eye stays in the possession of the bride, and is ultimately passed to the next generation. It has always been so.'

'When you say always…'

He shrugged those impressive shoulders. 'No one knows for sure. Since some time in the sixteenth century, most probably. Or so the experts believe.'

The sixteenth century. Hell!

He didn't need to spell out the implications. She knew all about the value of ancient treasure. The reverential, almost mystical importance attached to it by tradition. And Q'aroum, for all its modern gloss, held its traditions dear.

Belle had an awful feeling she was just beginning to understand how important and valuable a ransom had been paid for her life. The implications made her stomach roil.

She flopped back in her chair, her breathing short and ragged. She fought for calm. For common sense.

'But everyone must realise you didn't hand it over as a bride price,' she reasoned. 'It's obvious the circumstances are completely different. And there was Duncan too. You paid the ransom for both of us.'

His eyes held hers, and the intensity of his unblinking gaze told her there was no easy way out. Her heartbeat thundered so loud in her ears she had to strain to hear his response.

'That is so. But you mustn't underestimate the importance of custom to my people. You've seen the new town, the wealth invested in education and modern infrastructure. Change is occurring, but Q'aroumis are slow to give up some things—such as their love of royal pomp and custom. That's one of the reasons I remain as head of state though we have a democratically elected parliament.'

He took another sip of thick black coffee with all the ease of a man discussing social trifles. But the hard lines of his face told their own story. This was no joke. He took it completely seriously.

'The circumstances are incidental.' His words were brusque. 'The fact is I gave up the necklace and I returned with you.' He shot her a look from under levelled black brows. Its intensity pinned her to her seat.

'To my people it is a simple equation. A bride gift in return for a woman. A ransom for a bride.'

His gaze brushed slowly across her face, igniting a curl of hot sensation deep inside her. As if he'd touched her, caressed her. And, despite this crazy situation, she couldn't prevent her instinctive, needy response.

She shook her head in denial. Of his words. Of the fierce, frightening heat building within her. She couldn't mistake it. It had been there when he spoke of al Akhtar men claiming their women. Stealing them from the high seas and making sure they never wanted to leave.

Excitement. That was what she felt. And desire.

The appalling realisation held her in frozen immobility as she stared back into his piercing eyes.

She didn't even *know* this man, yet some atavistic part of her psyche revelled in the idea of being claimed as his woman. Of belonging to him.

Her! A woman who'd made her way against the odds in a man's world. Who'd learned to be self-reliant at an age when other girls were dreaming of Prince Charming and happy-ever-after. She knew first hand that happy-ever-after was the stuff of fiction.

The sound of quick, measured footsteps cut across the thick web of tension enmeshing them. She blinked, had to make a physical effort to drag her eyes from Rafiq's compelling gaze. She turned to see Dawud approaching, dressed once more in army fatigues.

Immediately she sensed a new tension in Rafiq, though he said nothing, merely waited for the other man to approach.

'*Saba'a alkair*, Ms Winters,' Dawud said, with a slight, formal bow. 'I hope you are well rested.'

'*Saba'a alkair*, Dawud. Thank you, I'm well. And you?'

His gaze strayed to Rafiq, and she could have sworn some unspoken message passed between them.

'I am well, Ms Winters.' He paused. 'I come with urgent news for the Prince, if you'll permit?'

She wasn't sure whose permission he was asking, but she nodded.

He stepped closer and murmured to Rafiq. 'It is as you predicted, as we feared.'

'Where? When?' Rafiq's voice had a steely edge.

'Shaq'ara. Less than fifteen minutes ago.'

Belle watched Rafiq absorb the obviously unpalatable news. Emotion stripped his face to a mask of brooding severity. One hand clenched on the table. And then, in a single lithe movement, he stood before her.

'Forgive me, Belle. Important as our conversation is, we have something of an emergency on our hands. I must go.' As he spoke he gestured to Dawud, who nodded in her direction and then turned away, his footsteps quickening.

'We'll continue our discussion on my return. You will be patient and stay within the grounds until then?' He phrased it as a question, but it was unmistakably an order.

She scented danger in his battle-ready stance, in his aura of barely restrained power, as if only the thinnest veneer of civilised behaviour masked a ruthless warrior ready for combat. Whatever had sparked the martial glint in his eye, she wanted no part of it. She'd wait here in secluded comfort for his return.

Then they could sort out this bizarre notion of him buying her with an ancient bridal token.

'I'll wait.'

'Good. Ask for anything you want. The staff will look after you.' And with that he was gone, striding purposefully down the colonnade.

As he disappeared into the shadows Belle pressed a shaky hand to her abdomen. Her stomach muscles clenched in painful spasm. She swallowed convulsively, recognising too well the dry, rusty taste on her tongue. Rafiq's alert warrior stance had brought apprehension rushing back in a wave so potent she felt ill.

But this time the dread was different. She wasn't scared for herself. Her fear was for the enigmatic man who'd saved her life. The man who set her heart racing out of control every time she saw him. Who'd destroyed her comfortable illusions about her self-sufficiency, her needs as a woman, and her self-control. The man who, after a few short days, meant more to her than any man ever had.

By evening Belle couldn't sit still. She'd prowled the gardens, trying to concentrate on the lush tropical blooms. But they'd reminded her of the sensuous heat in Rafiq's eyes as he'd watched her this morning. She'd visited the royal reception rooms, been awed by a wealth so immense that the very walls of the main audience chamber were studded with jewels. But none were as dazzling as Rafiq's smile last night when he'd coaxed her, tricked her into staying here.

She had investigated an armaments room, its walls set with a bristling display of antique scimitars, muskets and other deadly weapons. But her frisson of unease had been less to do with that evidence of Q'aroum's violent past than with the memory of Rafiq's story. Of how his ancestor had stormed a passing ship and boldly abducted a woman simply because she'd pleased his eye. A woman he'd kept in the harem where Belle had slept.

But in her mind it was Rafiq on the deck of that ship. Rafiq with his feet planted wide, his muscled arms bare, his eyes gleaming with purpose and promise as he spied his prize: the woman he would take for his own.

And, of course, to Belle's despair, that woman was herself.

Sternly she told herself not to worry, that her fantasy had a sort of strange logic, given his stories of pillage, her own abduction and his role as her saviour. And even more so now, with his news of the royal betrothal token.

That titbit of information had stunned her. But she was sensible enough to know that, despite tradition, a man like Rafiq couldn't really expect or want marriage to someone like her. She was no princess but an ordinary hard-working Australian. A foreigner. Neither glamorous nor exotically beautiful. She guessed Rafiq would require both those qualities in a wife. And so, somehow, they'd find a way out of this betrothal business.

Yet put all those factors together and was it any wonder she'd spent the day picturing herself as his—what? His prize? His bride? *His woman.*

A tremor of terrible excitement, of wanting, shivered through her.

Belle stared blindly across the lamp-lit sitting room and tried to reassure herself. She was recuperating from the kidnap. She was under stress. It was all perfectly logical. Nothing to fret over.

Except there was more to this than some swashbuckling fantasy. There was a connection between them unlike anything she'd experienced. There was need—so strong it rocked her to realise how much she wanted to be near him, to be his.

Admitting that to herself took all her courage.

And there was more too. Far more than physical desire. That was why these slow-moving hours had edged her to the point of snapping.

The anxiety she'd felt for him hadn't eased. As the sun rose high in the sky, then dipped to the horizon she told herself he was safe. There was no danger. He was head of state, and the Q'aroumis wouldn't take chances with the life of their beloved prince.

But she remembered how he'd deliberately endangered himself in order to save her. And the adamantine set of his shoulders, the uncompromising angle of his jaw when he'd left this morning. Instantly the rushing swoop of fear began again, churning her stomach and drying her throat.

She had to find something to distract her from this sickening tension.

She'd already rung home. Spent an hour on the line talking to her mum, reassuring her again that there was no need for a trip to Q'aroum now she was safe. She'd spoken to Rosalie too, her heavily pregnant sister. Rose had sounded better than she had in months, as if she'd come to terms with her impending single parenthood.

Belle promised herself that soon, after the birth, she'd organise some time off from the expedition so she could visit her family.

She paced the room, too wound up to settle with a book or magazine. Her eye lit on an ornately carved rosewood screen at one wall. Sure enough, it slid aside to reveal a huge plasma screen television. She was flicking through the array of international cable channels when an image caught her eye and she stopped, transfixed.

It was a local news item. She didn't understand the reporter's excited Arabic, but she did understand the English subtitle. Shaq'ara. Where Rafiq had gone so many hours ago.

Her mouth dried as she stared at a huge crater in a wide street. Debris lay all around, the mangled wrecks of vehicles, the shattered remains of a shopfront. Then images of ambulances speeding along a road, sirens blaring.

An icy shiver of horror rippled through her. The images were all too familiar these days. A bomb blast. That was all it could be.

But in Q'aroum? She shook her head in disbelief. The country was renowned for its stability.

The scene changed abruptly to a close-up of two men. One old and bearded, his head swathed in an elaborate turban. He reached out to another man who clasped his arm.

Rafiq! For a moment she hadn't recognised him, wearing long, traditional Q'aroumi robes and with his head covered in a simple white headdress. But she couldn't mistake that commanding profile or the assertive jaw. Even on film Rafiq made her stomach clench and her pulse stutter.

In front of the two men a crowd of people had gathered, arms raised in applause, chanting something. She thought she heard Rafiq's name repeated several times.

Frustrated, Belle switched off the television and resumed her pacing. Whatever had happened in Shaq'ara, the main town on the nation's second most populous island, Rafiq was needed there to support and comfort his people.

Anxiety bit harder now. He'd deliberately walked into a dangerous and volatile situation. There could be no guarantees of his safety.

Of course that wouldn't have mattered to him. She understood him enough to realise he had an ingrained sense of duty: he wouldn't think twice about his safety if others were at risk. As hers had been four days ago. Not for him the option of command from a distance.

That should have impressed her. Yet she felt nothing but churning apprehension. Would he come back alive?

Belle had all but worn a track in the luxurious antique carpets when, around eleven o'clock, she heard a swift, sure stride she recognised. Her heart thumped in her throat and she swung round towards the door.

He paused in the doorway, filling her vision. He was dressed as she'd seen him on the television, in long pale robes over boots and trousers, with a heavily embroidered vest that made him look exotic and utterly romantic. The headdress was gone and his dark hair was pulled back, accentuating the bold interplay of bone and muscle that made up his aristocratic face.

He looked spectacular.

'Rafiq!' Her voice was a hoarse croak. 'Are you all right?'

'Of course I'm all right, Belle. Why aren't you in bed? Is something wrong?' His gaze sharpened, laser-bright, and she felt it graze her skin.

'No, nothing's wrong.' She paused to catch her breath. Her breathing was short and shallow, as if she'd been sprinting. Her skin prickled. 'No one seemed to know when you'd be back. I was…worried.'

Embarrassed, she dropped her gaze, then gasped and surged forward, her hand outstretched. 'You're injured.' She pointed to the splash of blood on one wide sleeve.

Rafiq held up his arm and looked at the stain, frowning, then shook his head. 'Not me, little one. I've been visiting people in hospital.'

'The bomb blast,' she whispered, and his eyes met hers, dark now, like the chill depths of an abyss.

'You know about that?'

'It was on the television news.'

He reached out and closed his hand around hers. His heat seeped into her skin, his hard strength supporting her. But she suspected it was he who needed the support, though he'd never admit it. It must have been a harrowing day.

It didn't matter that he was the Sovereign Prince of Q'aroum, fabulously wealthy and lord of all he surveyed. Right now he was simply Rafiq, the man who'd saved her, protected her, who needed solace. She ignored the inner voice that warned he'd become far too important to her in a few short days. That her relief at his arrival was out of all proportion to the circumstances.

She squeezed his fingers and drew him across the room to a wide sofa padded with embroidered silk cushions.

'You look exhausted,' she said. It was a lie. He looked fit and invincible, but his eyes were shuttered. He let her lead him and then sat down, watching her as she settled at the other end of the sofa, facing him.

'Tell me about it,' she said.

He shook his head. 'It is not suitable for you to hear.'

'Because I'm a woman?'

That made him smile, a crooked lifting of one side of his mouth in a twist of amusement that sparked a flare of heat deep inside her.

'How prickly you are, Belle. Why are you so ready to take offence? Don't you know it's the way of Q'aroumi men to protect their womenfolk?'

A forbidden thrill skated through her at the idea of Rafiq protecting her because she was his.

Absurd. She was her own woman; she didn't need a man to take care of her.

Yet the thrum of awareness vibrating through her body told another story.

Rafiq leaned back and watched the flicker of emotions across her face. He shouldn't enjoy her company quite so much. If he had any sense he'd send her to bed with a quick apology for his late return. But when he'd seen the unguarded emotion in her face, the concern and relief, and the yearning, he hadn't been strong enough to deny himself this small pleasure.

'But I'm not a Q'aroumi woman,' she said at last with the glimmer of a smile. 'I think I can bear to hear about your day.' She paused and her gaze dropped. 'If you want to talk about it.'

Rafiq watched her concentration as she plucked at the hem of her shirt. With her downbent head and restless hands she looked almost shy. What was going on in that beautiful head? Bellé was many things, but not bashful.

'Someone detonated a bomb in the city of Shaq'ara. We were fortunate no one was killed. But several people are in hospital, badly wounded.'

She frowned, looking up to snare him with that stunning azure gaze. Once again he felt its impact deep in his gut. He should be used to that by now, but it always stopped his breath for an instant. A fatal instant that inevitably made him wonder how it would feel if Belle did more than just look.

'It wasn't a suicide bomber, then?'

He shook his head. 'These people don't have such strength of conviction. They call themselves fundamentalists, fighting for a return to traditional values, but they're simply opportunists. Criminals seeking power.' His cousin Selim's idea of a return to traditional ways was the abolition of democracy and the installation of himself as autocratic ruler. It would mean utter ruin for the country as Selim stripped it bare. The very idea left a bitter taste in Rafiq's mouth.

Selim had to be stopped, and soon. No matter what the cost. The peace and the prosperity of Q'aroum were at stake.

'Who was the old man you were with, in front of the huge crowd?' Belle interrupted his turbulent thoughts.

He focussed on her as she leaned close, concern etched on her lovely face. Her hair was pushed back behind her ears, but it glowed like gold in the lamplight. Her wide, cerulean eyes dazzled like jewels. But it was her mouth that drew him. She had the lips of a *houri*, voluptuous and tempting. The sort of lips that held untold promise for a man wearied by violence and suffering.

And suddenly the uncertainty that had plagued him for days vanished. A weight lifted off his shoulders as he shed the unaccustomed doubt. His way forward was obvious—so simple it was extraordinary he'd prevaricated so long. He only had one option if he wanted to protect his people. And, as their sheikh, he must take it.

'The terrorists claim they're committed to bringing back the old ways. They pretend they're acting with the sanction of revered community elders, but that's a lie. I met publicly today with several of the most respected community leaders in Shaq'ara, and they made it clear they would never support those who use violence.'

She nodded, her eyes meeting his. Rafiq felt the familiar thickening of his blood as their gazes meshed, the pooling of need low in his body. He faced the truth: he would enjoy doing his duty. It was what he wanted, after all. That was why he'd rejected the idea initially: because it so exactly concurred with his own, thoroughly selfish desires.

'They're trying to destabilise the country through violence. We foiled a bomb attack on the markets only last week.' He shook his head. 'And, to my shame, they're led by a kinsman of mine. A distant cousin who'd become sheikh if he could, and rule Q'aroum as his own personal domain.'

Her brows furrowed. 'But if he's a distant cousin, how could he—?'

He spread his hands, palm up. 'The title of sheikh is passed by direct inheritance, but very occasionally, in times of great need or bad leadership, the title can pass to another male of the al Akhtar family. It would be decided by a council of elders.'

Selim still had an immense way to go before he could hope to sway the council. Obviously he thought a campaign of terror might achieve what a personal approach could not. But how Q'aroum would suffer in the meantime.

'Your kidnap was part of Selim's scheme. The abduction and death of two foreign nationals would put immense pressure on the government. And the ransom was a key part of his strategy.'

She frowned, obviously weighing up his words. 'I can understand that our kidnapping might trigger an international incident.
But the government couldn't be held to blame. And why that
ransom? Why not ask for cash they could use to buy guns?
Surely that would be easier to handle than an antique necklace?'

He nodded. 'The Peacock's Eye is much more than a
necklace. It holds a special place in local folklore. It's intimately associated with the al Akhtar dynasty and the belief that
my family is destined to rule.' He saw her eyes widen.

'To you, Belle, such ideas may be quaint, but here they're
taken very seriously indeed. The loss of the Eye reflects on the
prestige of the royal house. And on my fitness to lead.' His voice
deepened as he thought of his father, his grandfather, and their
unstinting efforts to drag Q'aroum into the modern world.

He would *not* fail them.

'My country has only been a democracy for thirty years.' He
saw her nod, and hoped that meant she might understand. 'Many
still cling to the belief that the Sheikh is the natural leader, the
born ruler. As a result we have a system whereby power is
shared between parliament and the head of state. The stability
of the nation depends on that system working seamlessly.'

'And if it's disrupted?' Her voice was a whisper.

'The possibility of chaos.' He raised his hand as she opened her
mouth to speak. 'I don't believe it would come to that. The
Q'aroumis are a peaceful people, despite their colourful history.
And they can see the benefits of modern government. It would take
far more than a bomb blast for Selim to achieve what he wants.'

Which was why Rafiq's security experts were in such a
flurry of concern about his personal safety. An assassination
would solve so much for Selim.

'We've identified the conspirators and we're tracking them
down. They won't be at large for long.' He shot her another
look. 'The danger is what damage they could wreak in the

meantime. It's of paramount importance that there's no sign of weakness on the government's part. Or on mine.'

There was silence as she absorbed his words.

'What are you going to do?' she asked eventually.

His lips curved up in a smile. She really was perceptive. She knew him well enough to realise he wouldn't sit back and wait for events to unfold.

He reached out and took her hand in his, drawing her slowly, inexorably, along the sofa until the scented heat of her body warmed his. This was where she belonged, he decided. Here and nowhere else.

She swallowed, and he watched the convulsive movement of muscles in her slender neck. He wanted to reach out and touch her there, put his hand on the silken flesh he remembered from the night she'd lain beneath him. But for now he would content himself with her hand.

He turned it over so it rested palm up in his. He could feel the tiny tremors racing across her skin and knew that she recognised it too, the inevitable connection between them. Slowly, deliberately, he stroked his index finger across her palm and heard her breath escape in a hiss.

Yes, he would enjoy doing his duty.

And she would enjoy it too.

He lifted his gaze, satisfied at the glazed eyes, the hooded lids that revealed exactly what she was feeling.

'You're right, *habibti*. I must act.' Again he stroked her palm, and was rewarded by her immediate shudder of sensual reaction.

'The people believe you are my woman, that I gave up the Peacock's Eye for love of you. They would view any other explanation as a sign of weakness, something not to be tolerated in their prince.' He paused for the length of a heartbeat.

'I will make you my bride.'

CHAPTER SIX

Just as well she was sitting down.

The deep cadence of his voice echoed in her ears, seemed to magnify as her brain processed the simple, utterly incredible statement.

'You can't be serious!' Her eyes goggled. Belatedly she snatched her hand from his. She couldn't think when he touched her. Or when he looked at her so intensely that she imagined a lick of flame in his gaze. Like now.

'I would not joke about anything so serious.'

His stare held hers captive, and she recognised again the insidious ripple of arousal, of wanting deep inside. That scared her almost as much as the determination etched on Rafiq's aristocratic features.

'But that's impossible!'

He shook his head slightly, just enough to make his gold earring sway. 'Not impossible at all. All it takes is you and me, together.'

Belle clamped her lips to cut off the sound of her indrawn breath. He didn't mean *together* like that. He was talking about a political gesture. A ceremony to assuage his people's expectations.

'You know what I mean.' She shifted back on the wide divan, edging away from him. 'Marrying some woman just because you paid her ransom: the idea is ridiculous!'

He transformed before her eyes. From seductive intrigue to offended hauteur in an instant. He didn't perceptibly move but somehow he loomed closer, his powerful shoulders blocking the rest of the room from her vision. Or maybe it was the spark of outrage in his eyes, the anger in his flared nostrils and thinned lips, that made him suddenly so intimidating.

'There is nothing ridiculous in acting to preserve the safety of my people. As their sheikh, it is my duty to protect them.'

But not mine. She bit down on the words in case they slipped out.

'I didn't mean that.' She clenched her hands, forcing herself to meet his gaze. He projected an intimidating aura of power, of authority, honed, no doubt, by centuries of al Akhtar arrogance. But strangely she found it easier to defy him now, when he was annoyed, than when his smouldering sensual promise made her weak at the knees.

'I meant there must be another option. Some alternative to marriage.' Just saying the word brought goosebumps to her skin.

'If you have a suggestion I am, as ever, willing to hear it.' He tilted his eyebrows in enquiry.

'*I* don't know.' She spread her hands helplessly. 'I don't understand the situation well enough to suggest anything. But there must be some way out of this. Marrying a stranger in these circumstances is preposterous.'

Something shifted in his expression, something that made her want, more than anything, to escape. She didn't like the look in his eyes.

'We're hardly strangers, Belle.' His voice dropped deep, to a level of purring intimacy that shook her to the core.

Time was suspended, even the pulse beating in her ears seemed to slow and her blood congeal as she watched him lean close. His body heat radiated against her, his clean male scent filled her nostrils.

It took a supreme effort of will not to shrink away. Or tuck herself in against him. When he looked at her like that she was too tempted to believe he felt the same bone-deep attraction that had befuddled her since he'd burst into her life.

The problem was that he seemed the embodiment of every fantasy: strong, protective, intelligent, honourable...devastating. Too good to be true.

She snagged a desperate breath.

'But we're not in love.'

Oh, hell. Had she really been foolish enough to blurt that out? Heat climbed her throat as she met his scrutiny.

'Love?' he queried, one dark brow winging up in a face suddenly still and intent. 'You are in love with someone?'

For a moment the question hung between them: provocative, dangerous.

'No, no.' Damn! How had she got herself into this? It seemed that the harder she tried to find a way out of the quagmire the deeper she sank. 'There's no one. But I'd hoped...'

She stopped, appalled that she had to explain something so personal. Especially to Rafiq, who'd probably had potential brides paraded for his inspection since he was in his teens. A man who obviously viewed marriage as an arrangement of state, not a meeting of lovers.

Belle took a sustaining breath and lifted her chin. 'It's possible that one day I'll meet someone—'

'So! You would deny me, deny my country, this marriage because of a hope, a mere wish for the future?' His brows drew together in a ferocious scowl.

'You must know I'll do whatever I can to help. But *marriage*! Your people surely can't expect that. They must realise we've only known each other a few days.'

'And yet a few days can be enough to choose a bride.'

Something about his expression made her recall the story of

his piratical ancestor. She shook her head. She couldn't afford to be distracted now.

'And you'll find that, for all our strength and tenacity, we Q'aroumis have a strongly romantic streak. My people are curious at the idea of their sheikh giving up such a spectacular fortune for a woman. It appeals to their sense of the dramatic.' He paused, watching her intently. 'They believe I'd only relinquish such a precious treasure for the woman I love.'

Belle swallowed, then circled her dry lips with her tongue. What was it about this man that those simple words could rock her off balance?

'Then surely it's a matter of correcting their assumption.'

'That's one alternative, of course.'

'But not one you want to follow.' That much was obvious.

'You know a little of Q'aroum, Belle. You understand our blend of old traditions and new ways. As hereditary head of state, it's vital that I'm seen to embody the strength my people expect. The strength for which my family is renowned. During this crisis it's essential their trust is not shaken.'

He sat back and spread his palms wide.

'They're romantic enough to accept the idea of me acting out of love. But anything else—like handing over a national treasure to preserve the life of a stranger—could be construed as weakness.' His hands clenched into fists on his knees. 'And any perception of weakness would play right into Selim's hands. It would give him the opportunity he needs to build some level of support.

'*That* is the alternative, Belle. That is what I'm fighting to avoid.'

It all made a horrible sort of sense. She'd been in the country almost a month and knew he was right—the Royal Sheikh was revered. His prestige reflected directly on the nation.

And then there was what he'd left unsaid. That he hadn't

needed to save her. Most countries, including her own, had a policy of not negotiating with terrorists. Which meant no ransom would have been paid. If it had been left in the hands of diplomats and policy-makers she'd bet that she and Duncan would still be on that island. *Not* a thought she wanted to pursue.

Rafiq had broken with internationally accepted practice. He'd gone out on a limb, paid a king's ransom and put his own reputation at stake. To save her.

Belle's stomach plunged in freefall.

How could she refuse him?

Rafiq waited only until Belle had informed her family, then ordered the betrothal be announced next day. By midday crowds of well-wishers thronged the palace gates.

The announcement had been straightforward, though couched in the elegant terms favoured by the royal chamberlain. But the betrothal itself had been anything but simple, Rafiq decided ruefully as he dressed in his ceremonial robes.

What a woman he had chosen! He smiled at the memory of her last night, determination glittering in her eyes as she refused him. She'd protested and argued well into the early hours of the morning, finding so many reasons why their wedding was unnecessary.

If she didn't have such a passion for marine archaeology she'd have made a fine career as a lawyer, doggedly putting her case.

But of course the marriage was necessary, and so, eventually, she'd agreed.

Another man might have lashed out at her, his pride wounded at her initial rejection. But Rafiq saw beyond the surface. Saw it was the circumstances she railed against, not him.

Who wouldn't fight against a fate that ordained immediate marriage to a virtual stranger? Hadn't he, at the age of thirty-one, deliberately avoided marriage to any of the women who'd been so carefully brought forward for his approval over the years?

Belle was distressed at having her freedom curtailed. At having the decision taken out of her hands by necessity. Women wanted to be wooed and courted, to be made love to by a passionate man who promised them romance.

But Belle couldn't conceal the way she felt about him, he thought with satisfaction. Her body's responses mirrored his own desire for her: urgent, instant, undeniable. And in all the protests she'd made last night she hadn't once mentioned physical incompatibility.

His lips curved again into a slow smile as he thought of claiming her as his bride. Anticipation hummed through him, a palpable force. Just the thought of her did that to him.

It would be his duty to ensure Belle found pleasure in this union. As much pleasure as he intended to take from it.

He adjusted his wide ceremonial sash, embroidered with the twin al Akhtar emblems of falcon and peacock, as he contemplated the woman who waited for him. There was a spring in his step when he strode from the room.

Belle stood statue-still as the women clustered around her, chattering and adjusting her delicate silk robes with a tweak here and a stitch there. Surely it didn't take so many to dress her? But she didn't have the heart to spoil their pleasure.

It was clear that preparing the affianced bride of the Sheikh for her first public event was a great honour. And they were so genuinely happy for her, wishing her good fortune and pressing tiny personal gifts into her hands: a vial of rose perfume, a carved trinket box inlaid with mother of pearl, a posy of flowers.

But, despite the luxurious trappings, *being* the Sheikh's betrothed was anything but a fairytale.

She felt cold as ice. She'd barely slept, tossing and turning in her huge bed as she recalled last night's argument with Rafiq. His insistence that their marriage was a necessity.

Nothing she'd said had swayed him from his purpose.

Her whole life had been turned upside down. She would be tied to a man she barely knew. Would become a citizen of a country she'd been in for just four weeks.

And, despite his assurances, she doubted she could continue her career, exploring and mapping ancient shipwrecks, when she was a royal princess.

A bubble of hysterical laughter rose in her throat. She could just imagine it—her in a dive-suit with a couple of ladies-in-waiting up on the expedition vessel getting seasick while she worked. Their idea of treasure would be something golden and glittering and ornamental. Hers was a newly discovered style of amphora, or perhaps some tiny detail of ship construction and navigation gleaned from an ancient wreck.

And she'd be so far from home. Rafiq had been quick to promise her trips to Australia, visits from her family on his private jet. Yet there was a huge difference between living overseas to pursue a career and accepting that her new home would be thousands of kilometres from her family.

She'd almost hoped her mother would be so upset about the news that she'd have an excuse to renege on the deal.

Certainly her mum had been stunned. Curious and cautious, and more than a little taken aback. But after she'd heard Belle out she'd been understanding and supportive. That was typical of her level-headed mother, and what she should have expected, since she'd learnt stoic self-sufficiency and composure at her mum's knee.

Instead of getting hysterical, Maggie Winters had said she knew Belle was sensible enough to do what was best in the circumstances.

Sensible! Belle winced. She'd been anything but that these

past few days. Continually fantasising about Rafiq. Letting this passing infatuation cloud her judgement. She squeezed her eyes shut and let the women's flow of mingled Arabic and English wash over her.

Maybe this obsession was the result of too many years of hard work and common sense. She'd spent so long doing the right thing, not taking time for light-hearted flirtation or frivolity. Since the day her dad had walked out on them and she'd decided it was time to help her mum shoulder the family responsibilities.

How sensible was it to imagine this marriage could ever be more than a public show? Her cheeks washed with fiery heat as she remembered her dream only a few hours ago. Rafiq had pulled her close and declared that he wanted her for himself. Because he could never let her go.

How pathetic could she get? To secretly desire so much more. To want something…personal. Something…permanent.

But the marriage would be a fake. As soon as the political circumstances changed Rafiq would find a way to end it. He wouldn't burden himself by keeping a wife he didn't want.

Pain lanced her chest. Why did the idea hurt so much?

She wasn't herself, that was why. The counsellor at the hospital had spoken about the unsettled emotions she could expect after her traumatic experiences. Her feelings for Rafiq must be a legacy of that. He'd saved her. He was larger than life in every respect, handsome enough to take any woman's breath away, strongly protective and honourable. She'd built up a fantasy romance around him.

It was pure infatuation she felt for Rafiq. Infatuation and gratitude. She clung to the idea like a lifeline.

All she could do was play her part in public and hope these emotions wore off soon. Before she did something stupid, like let him see how she felt.

Something penetrated her circling thoughts. Silence. The

bright chatter stopped abruptly. She snapped her eyes open as a sudden tension filled the room.

Slowly she turned towards the door. But already she knew what she'd see. A sizzle of awareness told her Rafiq was there. It was as if she had an inbuilt radar that alerted her when he was near.

Sure enough, as the women curtsied she saw him stride into the room, eating up the space between them till the massive suite seemed unbelievably small and intimate. Her stupid heart fluttered out of rhythm. Her breathing shallowed.

Just because he was tall, dark and handsome, she told herself. And because he saved your life, she rationalised.

But would gratitude explain the melting sensation deep inside her? As if something vital had liquefied, turned into a hot, sweet ache that swirled and pooled lower and lower. It took all her will-power to stand her ground as he approached.

Belle snagged a breath and stared straight into his sea-green eyes. He really was extraordinarily handsome. And the way he looked at her, as if he saw no one but her, sent delicious anticipation skittering through her.

She broke eye contact and looked at the women, summoning up a smile of thanks.

This wouldn't do. She'd agreed to go through with this masquerade. But it would be a disaster if she kept reading things into his expression. Things that weren't there. To Rafiq she was the solution to a problem. That was all. Despite the warmth of his hand holding hers last night, and the deep honeyed tones that had sent an illicit shiver of excitement through her, she meant nothing to him.

She was simply reacting on the most basic level to an ultra-sexy man. A man, moreover, who had the sort of integrity and honesty she'd always admired.

Belle pushed back her shoulders and lifted her chin. The only way to get through this with her dignity and self-respect intact was to ignore the undercurrents and pretend he didn't affect her.

Rafiq said something in Arabic and the women curtsied again, then left with a few speculative glances over their shoulders. He turned and smiled at her, and she felt her heart turn over in her breast.

Hell! What hope did she have?

'You look exquisite, Belle.' He paced closer.

Heat bloomed beneath her skin at the compliment, and at the look on his face. She had to remember she was fooling herself when she saw hot possessiveness glitter in his eyes, sensual promise in the curve of his lips. She was doing it again: imagining what she wanted to see.

That knowledge gave her the strength to stand her ground. But when he took her hand in his, raised it to his mouth and kissed it, she couldn't prevent the tremor of desire that coursed through her. Or the jittering pulse that leapt to life in her throat.

Had Rafiq noticed? He stood so long, holding her hand to his mouth. His breath was a warm haze on her skin, his gaze searing as he watched her with those exotic green eyes. Belle's whole body heated in response, *willing* him to press his lips to her hand again. Praying he wouldn't.

'Thank you. And you look magnificent, Rafiq,' she managed at last. Her voice had a hoarse edge and she swallowed. 'Like a prince out of the *Arabian Nights*.'

He laughed. 'You are a romantic, Belle. I knew it.' He drew her close and tucked her arm through his. So close that the memories flooded back. Of his big body so hard and impressive, lying intimately over hers. Of the long hours spent cradling his head, his breath feathering against her neck. Of the way he made her feel: vulnerable, aware, needy. The sea-salt and musk scent of his skin tantalised her, awoke responses she'd rather ignore.

He led her to the door and Belle concentrated on maintaining some minuscule distance between them. But in these clothes, these sensuous, butterfly-sheer silks, she felt the whisper of temptation with every step she took.

'You are excellent for my ego,' he said. 'Every man likes to hear how wonderful he is. I see that in marrying you I have much to look forward to.'

Belle stumbled and his hand tightened on her arm. He stopped, the laughter fading from his face. She looked up to see his expression grow serious.

'It will be all right. I promise, Belle, you will have nothing to regret in this marriage. I will look after you.'

She nodded, snared by the strength of emotion she read in his face. The only problem was she knew he was wrong. Already she had nothing but regrets.

'I understand how difficult this is. And how much I'm asking of you.' His lips curved up in a tender smile that melted at least one of her vital organs. Maybe it was her lungs—she had to fight for breath just watching him.

'You will carry this off with dignity and grace. I will support you, and you will be a wonderful success.' His voice dropped to a low murmur that weakened her knees.

He leaned close as he spoke, his words caressing her face, and Belle bit down hard on her lip, fighting the compulsion to tilt her head up just a fraction more to close the distance between them. To press her lips against his and assuage the aching need that consumed her.

His eyes gleamed with an inner fire. His hands clamped tighter on hers. Drawing her closer or holding her away?

'I will not forget what you have done for my country.'

For his country. Right. A cold, solid lump of common sense thudded down inside her, smashing the shimmering tension, dousing the bright expectation that had swelled as she waited for his lips to take hers.

They were going through with this charade to save his country. *And don't you forget it, Belle. This is all for show.*

Apparently she managed to look the part of radiant bride-to-be, even though her stomach was a roiling mass of nervous tension and her smile a taut stretch of stiff muscles. When she emerged into the huge throne room on Rafiq's arm and took her place beside him, on a smaller ornate, glittering chair, there was no outcry, no protest from the audience that this was a sham.

The massive space was crammed to standing room only, and she could see the throng spilling out into a huge antechamber. It was like watching a wave as the crowd bowed low before their prince. And she felt the speculation in their eyes as they stared at her, whispering amongst themselves.

'Don't worry, Belle. All you need to do is follow my lead.' Rafiq sent her a smile that tripped her pulse. And then, suddenly, the chamberlain was in front of them, ushering forward the first of the people to be presented.

There were wealthy nobles in traditional clothes almost as gorgeous as her own gold-embroidered azure silk. There were men in suits and women in elegant Western-style dresses. And there were many more in less sumptuous clothes, obviously of more humble origins. All were welcome and all were treated attentively.

She didn't have to do anything except smile and nod. When the well-wishers spoke English, Rafiq encouraged her to speak for herself. But otherwise she was free to watch the interplay between the Sheikh and his people, and what she saw reassured her. There was genuine friendliness and respect on both sides. And no trace of anger or doubt in the faces of the people who came to see his promised bride.

She even became accustomed to receiving fulsome compliments, though she suspected Rafiq secretly enjoyed translating the more flamboyant ones for her. There was a glimmer of something that must be humour in his eyes as he watched her try not to blush.

Eventually he called a halt, telling the servants to direct the newcomers to the feast that had been prepared.

'Come,' he said, standing up and taking her hand. 'You need a break.'

Belle nodded, concentrating on appearing immune to his touch as he led her through an arched doorway and into a small sitting room that shimmered with gold and amber silks. A low table was set with platters of honey cakes and nuts, and dark purple grapes with the bloom of the vineyard still on them. Even better, the scent of fresh coffee wafted to her nostrils.

She breathed deep, suddenly realising how stiff she felt. They'd been in the audience chamber for hours. She rolled her shoulders and sank onto a plumply cushioned couch.

'How much longer will people keep coming?'

Rafiq settled himself on a divan opposite her and reached for the elegant coffee pot. He poured the steaming liquid into a tiny cup. 'Today is just the beginning. They'll keep arriving all week.'

'All *week*?' She was exhausted after just a couple of hours.

He looked up, snaring her with his sea-deep gaze that held so many secrets. 'Until the day we are wed.'

CHAPTER SEVEN

'*One week* till the wedding?' The bright honey-gold of her hair caught the light as she shook her head emphatically. 'That's impossible.'

Rafiq watched the hectic colour flare in Belle's cheeks, then fade. She'd said the same when he'd informed her of his decision to marry. *Impossible.* Perversely, her disbelief had spurred his determination to proceed.

Didn't she see there was no turning back now, whatever her doubts? There was too much at risk.

'It's the tradition, Belle. We don't believe in long betrothals here.' And for the first time he could appreciate the reasons for that custom. Now he'd decided to take Belle as his wife, the anticipation, the knowledge that she'd soon be his, threatened to overcome his scruples. It was increasingly difficult to keep his distance, knowing that he'd soon have exclusive rights of possession. The need to observe public protocols, such as the open audiences with his people, was a blessing in disguise. It kept him from acting precipitately when he knew she needed time to adjust to so many changes.

'Well, it's not tradition where I come from.' Her lips thinned into a mulish line and her chin jutted.

How could a woman's temper, her obstinacy, be so arousing?

He felt the heat build in his body as desire sparked. He wanted to haul her into his arms and kiss her till she didn't have the energy left to argue.

'I realise this is unfamiliar to you. That it's not as you would have planned your wedding.' A sharp pang of sensation stabbed deep in his chest at the idea of her back home in Australia, planning to marry some other man. Some man she'd convinced herself she loved. He thrust the idea away. 'But it's necessary that we preserve tradition. There should be no doubts that this wedding is genuine and in keeping with custom.'

'And I don't have any say in it at all?' Fire blazed from her azure eyes and Rafiq repressed a smile. Arguing with Belle was fast becoming one of his favourite pastimes. He looked forward to next week, when he could enjoy making up properly after a disagreement.

It was a relief to see her animated. She'd been as dazzlingly beautiful as ever this morning, elegant and graceful in her finery. But he'd had the unsettling notion that something vital was missing. That somehow she wasn't fully participating. He'd wondered if she was suffering delayed shock when he'd seen her so pale and tense, surrounded by a flock of women in her room. Her gaze had been almost vacant, and she'd moved like an automaton. He'd sought to reassure her, but he wasn't sure he'd succeeded.

'Of course you'll contribute to the arrangements. There will be much to decide.'

'And if I decide that I'd prefer a longer engagement?'

He shook his head. 'On that I can't negotiate. The very purpose of this marriage is to ensure continued stability. If we delay it will be assumed there's a problem. That the wedding is only a smokescreen.'

'Which it is.' She clasped her hands tight in her lap and tension radiated from every line of her body.

He remembered the coffee he'd poured and offered it to her. 'Here, you'll feel better when you've had something to eat and drink.'

She leaned forward and took the cup, averting her gaze from his. 'It will take a lot more than a meal to make me feel comfortable about this.'

'You've consented to marry me.' His voice dropped to a deep rumble. 'Are you saying you're going back on your word?' He frowned, surprised to discover how anxious he was to hear her confirm her promise.

'No, I'm not backing out,' she said at last, and then bit her lip. 'But surely we can delay a little?'

Rafiq leaned back, watching her intently, ignoring the rush of relief he felt at her words. 'The sooner we're wed the sooner the situation will calm. And the better for all concerned.'

Her eyes met his, and once again he felt a frisson of shock at their impact. It was like seeing a glimpse of paradise.

'We can discuss the details later, with my staff. In the meantime you need to think about who you'd like to invite to the celebrations. First we'll arrange to fly your family here. They'll stay in the palace, of course.'

She would enjoy planning that, having her family about her at such a time.

But the frown pleating her brow told another story.

'That won't be necessary,' she said, after a long pause.

'You don't *want* them here?'

'Of course I want them here.' Her eyes flashed fire at him before she looked down at her coffee and took a quick sip. 'But the timing is wrong. They can't attend.'

It sounded like an excuse. Who would not want to come to their daughter's wedding?

'My jet can be available to bring them at any time—'

'But they won't be able to attend.' She put her cup down on the table with a click. 'My sister is expecting a baby.'

'My felicitations. It must be a happy and exciting time for her.'

Belle raised her eyes to his and for a moment he read anguish in her expression. Then she blinked and her expression went blank. What was going on here?

'Thank you. But there are complications. Rosalie's condition isn't as good as it should be, and she's not allowed to travel, especially with the birth so soon. She's under doctor's orders for strict bed-rest.'

Ah, now he understood. Obviously the sisters were close, and Belle was distressed that Rosalie couldn't attend. 'We'll arrange for her to visit as soon as she's able,' he assured her. 'For as long as you wish. But in the meantime your parents will want to be here for the wedding.'

She shook her head. 'I'm afraid not. There's only my mother now, and she's caring for Rosalie.'

Silently Rafiq cursed himself for blundering into her grief. The last thing he wanted was to cause her pain.

'I'm sorry, Belle. I hadn't realised your father was dead. You were very close?' He still remembered the utter shock of losing his own parents in an air crash when he was little more than a child.

She shrugged, and he saw the jerky stiffness of taut muscles in the movement. There was a twist to her beautiful mouth. 'I thought we were. Until he walked out and left us without a word.'

Bitterness laced her words. It was obvious her pain hadn't healed.

Rafiq could only imagine how hurtful it must be to face such rejection. He wanted to go to her, pull her close and comfort her. Yet her brittle composure seemed so fragile. He knew instinctively that she wouldn't welcome such an advance.

'Was this recent?'

She shook her head. 'No, it's ancient history now. He left the day before my twelfth birthday.'

Yet the scars of that hurt lingered. How betrayed she must have felt. Especially at such an impressionable age.

He felt a surge of protectiveness so strong it staggered him. How could her father have treated her in that way? Abandoned his family, his responsibilities, the people who cared for him?

Rafiq watched her reach for a plate and help herself to an assortment of fruit and nuts. She looked unconcerned, her movements quick and smooth. But the tension hadn't left her. She looked too composed. Almost rigid in her control.

Inevitably it set him wondering if her father's disloyalty might account for her fierce independence. She was more staunchly self-sufficient than any woman he'd met. It was one of the things that drew him to her. Now he speculated on whether that trait had grown out of pain and grief. In many ways Belle was an enigma to him. But one he was determined to solve.

'I lost my parents when I was eleven,' he said, in an attempt to bridge the silent gulf between them. Her head swung abruptly round towards him and he saw the flash of compassion in her expression. 'They were in a chopper, coming back from a visit to one of the outlying islands.'

He still remembered the perfect cloudless blue sky that afternoon as he'd waited for them to return.

'It should have been a routine flight, but something went wrong. A mechanical failure. There were no survivors.'

'Oh, Rafiq! To lose them *both* like that.' Her eyes were sympathetic. At least the haunted look in them had disappeared.

'I had my grandfather. He brought me up. And I count myself lucky for that. He was a great man.'

'I'm sure he was.' Then she staggered him with her first compliment. 'He did a fine job. I'm sure he'd be proud of you now.' A tiny evocative smile curved her lips.

He inclined his head, surprised to discover how much her words warmed him. How important they were to him.

'I'm honoured that you think so. And I'm convinced that your mother is a very special woman, to have produced a daughter like you.'

He watched, satisfied, as a blush of colour warmed her cheeks. He hated seeing her look bereft, as she had a moment ago. Even when fighting off exhaustion and terror she'd never looked as lost as she had when talking of her father.

'I'll look forward to meeting her in person.' He paused. 'In the meantime, I'd very much like to speak with her before the wedding.' To pay his respects and to set her mind at ease that he would do all within his power to look after her daughter.

'I'm sure she'd appreciate that.' Belle's expression was wary.

'Good. It's time I spoke with her. Very soon now we'll be family.'

Six days later Belle's world changed for ever.

In front of thousands of Q'aroumis she wed their sovereign prince. Millions of people around the globe, her own family included, watched television footage of the royal pair receiving the congratulations of their people. And heard the resounding cheers as the massive crowd roared its approval.

None of it had seemed real to Belle. Until now.

Finally, as nearby a clock chimed midnight, she found herself alone with Rafiq for the first time all day.

Cinderella time. Time for the world to change back to normal.

But as she stared across the private salon into the compelling eyes of the man she'd just married, Belle knew her life would never be the same again. That was when she realised she was in trouble.

He regarded her steadily. Too steadily. His assessing gaze tore at her façade of composure, leaving her nervous. Her breathing was shallow, her palms damp.

All day she'd played her part, model bride—first at a Q'aroumi then at a Western wedding ceremony. She'd stood at Rafiq's side through the interminable photo session, and again at the official reception, where locals and foreign dignitaries had clustered around, congratulating, assessing, speculating.

And now they were alone. The sense of unreality that had buoyed her through the sumptuous proceedings splintered as Rafiq paced towards her.

This was no illusion. She had bound herself to him.

Scorching darts of apprehension jabbed her, hot and unsettling. Her abdomen churned from the surge of adrenaline that spasmed through her muscles.

Fear?

Or anticipation?

As he closed the distance between them she focussed on the clear green of his eyes. And what she read there snatched her breath away.

Even dressed in a traditional bridal gown, with its full-length, concealing folds, she felt more vulnerable than when she'd knelt before him that first time, wearing only a Lycra swimsuit and manacles. Then he'd been her saviour, determined yet gentle in his role as rescuer.

But now his gaze was hot, possessive. His eyes sparked with the blaze of ownership, searing her to the core.

She backed a step and he paused, eyes narrowing.

'You must be tired. It's been a long day for both of us.' His deep voice hadn't changed. Smooth as fine chocolate, dark as temptation, it swirled around her, inviting her to relax, terrifying her with its seductive power.

'Would you help me?' He raised his hands to the vivid white cloth of his headdress and tugged one end free. His lips curved in a wry smile that banished the image of predatory, stalking male. Had it been an illusion?

'Of course.' Better to be doing something, anything, than stand and wonder what she'd just got herself into.

She ignored the luxurious shushing of her heavy satin dress as she walked, the weight of a solid gold collar around her throat. Satins and silks, luxury and jewels—they were all part of the fairytale display of a royal wedding. They didn't change her. She was clever, capable, a career woman from another world. All she had to do was remember it.

Belle avoided his gaze as she reached up and took the soft linen in her hands. Deftly he unwound its length, and just as quickly she folded it, concentrating on the simple task, avoiding his eyes. But his breath was warm against her face and the heat of his body was an encompassing aura. The scent of him, musk and sunshine, teased her senses.

His regard was like a touch, physical, unmistakable. It brushed over her face, lingering on her mouth, sweeping down her throat to the magnificently barbaric necklace she wore, and further, to the tight bodice of her gown.

With her arms raised, her body leaning infinitesimally towards him, she felt exposed. But she wouldn't react, she told herself, ignoring the swelling sensation of her breasts against the smooth satin.

Almost done. She snatched the last of the cloth from Rafiq's hands and stepped back, folding it neatly with fingers that barely quivered.

'Thank you, Belle.'

She looked at him then, and her pulse stuttered in shock. Instead of pulling his hair back in a sleek ponytail, as usual, Rafiq had left it unbound. Now it cascaded to his shoulders, a gleaming dark invitation to touch.

Her hands clenched on the wad of linen as she sucked in a desperate breath.

It should have looked effeminate, that shining mass of hair, or at least out of place on a man with such a starkly handsome face. But it didn't. Somehow it was the perfect foil for his solid jaw, his forceful nose and the deep slashes beside his mouth.

His mouth. Belle stared, ensnared by the sensuality of his lips. Knowing she should look away but unable to do it.

'And now we are wed.' His smile was pure satisfaction.

She shrugged. 'Officially.'

He shook his head and ebony hair spilled across his shoulders. 'Officially. But also legally, morally. Completely. It's done, Belle. Don't hide from the truth.'

Her eyes widened. 'The truth is that we married for political reasons. For the security of Q'aroum. To prevent an uprising that could cripple the country.'

'You sound like Dawud and my ministers.' His brows drew together. "Act quickly to prevent bloodshed. Remind everyone that the royal house of Akhtar is strong. Marry to buy time while we smoke out the rebels who'd destroy our democracy."'

'And that's exactly what you've done.'

'Yes. But is that all?' His voice was a seductive murmur that brushed across her skin as he stepped close.

She shivered.

'You're mine, Belle.' His fathomless gaze held hers in thrall. 'You gave yourself to me today. Not only legally, on paper. But in the flesh.'

She heard her breath hiss between her teeth, the blood throb in her ears. He couldn't have said what she thought he'd said.

'You belong to me.' He lifted his hand and stroked his fingers along her cheekbone, down her neck, to splay possessively over the wide jewelled collar that sat like a brand on her skin. Her flesh tingled at the contact, forbidden desire skittering through her.

She heaved a deep, panicked breath. 'No! I don't—'

'Just as I belong to you, Belle.' He leaned close, his gaze

mesmerising. 'I'm all yours. Do you not enjoy the idea? The power that gives you?'

Bewildered, she stared at this man who'd swept into her life with the force of a swirling desert wind, who'd taken control of her future, her very person. She should be outraged. She *was* outraged. Surely it was anger that fizzed in her veins, heightening each sense, alerting her to every tiny movement of his big body.

Or was it anticipation?

Belle shook her head. She'd married to help him protect his people. That was the only reason. Wasn't it? She'd found him wildly attractive from the first, but she knew he was off-limits and had fought this infatuation with all her strength. She couldn't have persuaded herself into this position because she wanted him.

Could she?

Her brain was so befuddled by the realisation that Rafiq apparently wanted *her* that she couldn't think straight. How had it happened? When? She'd been convinced she was the only one affected by this lightning blast of need. Her blood sizzled with the realisation that she'd been wrong. The way Rafiq's gaze devoured her made it clear he saw more than political necessity in this situation.

'You're a strong woman, Belle. Too strong to hide from the truth.' His hand, heavy and knowing, slid across her heated flesh, exploring the neckline of her gown, turning her blood molten.

With his other hand he reached down and enfolded her hand in his long fingers, lifting it to press against the hot skin of his jaw. She felt the fine haze of heat, the slight abrasion where his beard would grow if he let it.

She tensed, registering the dart of pure fire that arrowed straight to her womb, spreading delicious, wanton heat between her legs and up to her burgeoning nipples.

'Rafiq.'

He shook his head, so close she saw her reflection in his eyes. 'Don't lie, Belle. It doesn't befit you.'

He dragged her hand across his mouth, licking the centre of her palm. A shock of desire ripped through her, holding her spellbound. He did it again, the gesture slow and intimate. Half-closed lids now hooded the bright awareness of his eyes. In that instant Belle knew she wasn't fighting him, but herself.

'Don't be afraid, *habibti*.' His words vibrated against her sensitive palm. 'You can reach out right now and take whatever you want.'

He drew her hand away from his mouth and lifted his other hand from her body to stand, arms akimbo, watching her. 'If you have the courage,' he whispered.

It was a taunt. A dare she'd be a fool to accept. But, heaven help her, right now her senses were singing with awareness of this sexy, stubborn, outrageous man.

She tried to remember all the reasons it would be a mistake to get too close to him. Self-preservation, that was one. There was danger in letting him discover her desperate need. Danger in revealing how much she wanted him. Because one day she'd have to walk away from him when this marriage was annulled. And when she did she couldn't afford to leave with a shattered heart. She had to preserve her distance, her sanity. Her dignity.

One day soon she'd recover from this infatuation.

His eyes met hers, enticing, daring her to act on impulse. Challenging her to acknowledge the smoking-hot desire that shimmered between them.

One kiss. Just one to satisfy her curiosity. After all she'd been through surely she deserved that much? It was so tempting to throw caution and common sense to the winds.

Her nostrils flared as she caught his intoxicating scent. A ripple of awareness shivered through her.

She should play safe. She'd been strong for so long. Surely she could do it for a little longer?

There was a flutter of white as his linen headscarf slipped from her fingers and streamed to the floor.

And with it went the last of her self-possession.

She gave in to the inevitable.

Slowly, deliberately, her heart thudding, she lifted her hands up over his wide shoulders to cradle the back of his head. The sensuous silk of his hair was pure decadence in her hands. Gulping a quick breath, she leaned up and into him on tiptoe, bringing her body against the solid heat of his lean torso. Belle almost stopped then, savouring the delicate frisson of awareness where they touched.

She was nervous, absurdly so. But she wanted more, and now, finally, her need overrode the desperate voice of warning in her brain. She wanted this so badly. She'd lost the power to deny herself any longer.

His lips were smooth, surprisingly soft beneath hers. He tasted like desire. Closing her eyes, she concentrated on learning the shape of his mouth, caressing its edges. She pressed her mouth to his, tugging at his bottom lip till he opened for her and she delved in to stroke her tongue tentatively against his.

She shuddered with delight as he responded, gently teasing and retreating. Tantalising her with an expertise that should have set off alarm bells. But the sensations were too heady for sensible thought.

Belle pressed herself closer to the hard male body beneath the fine cotton of his robe, revelling in the restrained power of his solid frame. Her hands tightened on his skull as she stretched up to deepen the kiss, but while he accommodated her caress, even kissed her gently back, he didn't let go. Not the way she craved.

'Kiss me properly,' she demanded against his lips as frustration surged in a red-hot tide. She pulled back a fraction to meet his eyes. 'Please, Rafiq.'

Her body throbbed with unfulfilled need. Surely it wasn't too much to ask—just one proper kiss?

Belle watched his lips slowly curve up in a smile of satisfaction that deepened the sexy grooves beside his mouth. A dangerous smile. Her heart thudded a rapid tattoo of exhilaration and trepidation. His eyes darkened, a possessive glitter igniting in them as his arms wrapped round her, binding her tight against him.

Yes! This was what she craved. She sighed as he bent his head to hers.

Everything about this kiss was different. The searing energy that pulsed between them, the erotic stroke of his tongue in her mouth that made her shudder in response. His masterful stance as he bent her back against his iron-hard arms, the spiralling tension that twisted faster, tighter, more urgently with every beat of her racing pulse. He took control of the kiss with the deliberate passion and seductive expertise she'd sensed in him from the first.

Dazedly she gave herself up to a sensuous embrace that made her forget everything except the desire throbbing between them. Her whole body flamed as he made love to her with his mouth, his hands, his whole being. The sensations were exquisite and shattering. She felt as if he bound her to him: body, mind and soul.

She was melting, clinging to him as he absorbed her essence with his kiss. And gave her in return more than she'd ever dared hope for.

Eventually he lifted his head. The blaze of sensual exhilaration she saw in his eyes trapped her gaze and stopped her breath. Gone was the polite distance, the discipline and the control that had marked his every action. Instead his expression was fiercely intense, searing her with its potency.

A thrill of primitive excitement coursed through her.

'I thought you'd never ask, *habibti*. You are the most stubborn woman I know.'

In one swift, lithe movement he bent and lifted her boneless form into his arms. His heat was all around her, binding her close, so she felt the thud of his heart, the rise and fall of his chest, the power of his muscle-hard body.

'And you're all mine,' he murmured with a growling, masculine satisfaction that brought her back to shocked reality with a sudden nerve-splintering jolt.

He turned and strode across the room, carrying her towards the wide, luxurious divan that filled one wall.

CHAPTER EIGHT

RAFIQ felt her stiffen. Silently he cursed himself for giving voice to the rampant possessiveness that had torn at his precarious control all day.

He'd fought to repress it, to act as a civilised man. But it had been a losing battle ever since he'd seen her wearing that distinctive gold and diamond collar, symbol of their marriage. Of his ownership.

From that moment she'd been his. It wasn't the wedding ceremony that bound them, or the public congratulations of their people. It was the sight of her, adorned by al Akhtar gold, her eyes skimming away as she placed her hand in his. Her fingers had been cool, trembling, and he'd felt a surge of triumph so strong it had rocked him. And underlying it was an even more powerful desire to protect. She'd put her life in his hands, and he wouldn't fail her.

He'd barely been able to restrain the surge of sexual need that roared through him. Only by retreating into the safety of rigid decorum had he been able to keep his hands off her. To get through the day's interminable formalities without dragging her into the nearest unoccupied room and taking her with all the urgency of his escalating desire.

Now she was *his*. That kiss had sealed it. Exhilaration fizzed in his blood and tightened his muscles.

Shimmering satin moulded the sleek curves of her slim body. Its sheen was like water on priceless pearls, accentuating her allure. He'd take exquisite delight in stripping it off her—soon.

But now it seemed there was one more hurdle to overcome. Belle still fought her destiny.

'Rafiq!' Her voice was husky, drawing heat to his taut lower body. 'Put me down.'

Just what he had in mind. The divan in this suite was enormous, and soft enough to cradle her body. Personally he wouldn't have cared if they'd had only a carpeted floor, or even the desert sand, at their disposal. As long as he could lose himself in her.

Ignoring the compulsion to hurry, he lowered her gently to the divan, positioning himself to lie beside her, propped on one elbow.

Her hair flared bright as gold over the silk coverlet, and the fresh, sweet scent of her filled his senses. Her breasts rose and fell with an arousal she couldn't hide, despite the anxiety in her wide eyes.

He pressed his palm to the neckline of her gown, luxuriating in the feel of her bare hot flesh. So soft, so delicate. She'd be like that all over, her skin like the velvet of a rose petal. He drew his hand down over the tightly fitted fabric till his palm centred on the nub of one nipple. She gasped as he slowly twisted his hand and a jolt of pure sexual need juddered through him.

His wife was so responsive, so passionate. The pulse of her arousal echoed the throb of his erection.

'Rafiq, no!' It was a thread of sound, a weak remnant of her normal firm tones. He smiled, knowing this last hurdle was all but overcome.

'Belle, yes,' he breathed against her ear, flicking his tongue against her neck, tasting her unique sweetness. She trembled as he pressed his lips to her jaw, the corner of her mouth. She groaned, and he felt the rigidity in her legs as he shifted his thigh over hers.

He dragged in a harsh breath. Control. He needed to slow the pace lest he simply tear the dress apart and take her hard and fast, ravage her like some barbarian.

Already his body pushed against hers. His erection was hard against her hip as he slid his leg right across her, imprisoning her thighs with his.

Yes! He'd been waiting a lifetime for this.

He cupped her jaw with his hand, feeling the telltale throb of her pulse against his fingers. Her eyes were huge as she stared up at him.

'We can't do this,' she whispered. 'We have to stop.'

He shook his head and watched her eyes fix on the fall of his hair around his shoulders.

'We can't stop this now, Belle.'

'But you don't really want me. I'm just a political necessity. This marriage is for show.'

Rafiq would have laughed if his face hadn't been drawn into aching tightness by the force of a need that bordered on desperation. His response was to shift his weight so that he lay, centred over her, pressing himself into the intimate heat of her, revelling in the way her thighs automatically edged apart to cradle him through the layers of their clothes. This was right—for both of them. She couldn't deny that.

'Is this for show, do you think?' he rasped from a raw throat. 'The way our bodies already welcome each other?'

She shook her head, squeezing her eyes tight shut. He read real distress in her face. It was like a douche of cold water against his burning skin.

He slid his finger gently over the luscious line of her bottom lip, stroking rhythmically till she opened her eyes and met his gaze.

'Why do you fight the inevitable, Belle? You belong to me. You know it's the truth. Your body knows it even as your mind fights it.'

There was a flicker of something in her eyes, a softening, an awareness that sent a surge of elation through his blood. Then he saw the way her jaw clenched, recognised that determined expression. She'd worn that look on the island, when she'd fought in desperation with the last ounce of her will-power.

'We're attracted,' she said. 'But that's all.'

That's all! Rafiq couldn't believe his ears. That she could dismiss what was between them so easily! She couldn't be that naïve, could she?

No matter. He had no intention of spending his wedding night anywhere but in his bride's bed.

'We've been thrown together by circumstance,' she continued, looking over his shoulder as if she couldn't bear to meet his eyes.

'Let me show you how much this has to do with circumstance,' he murmured, dropping his hand from her jaw to her breast. 'And how much it has to do with *us*.'

Her nipple was hard beneath his hand and he felt her breast thrust up into his touch. Belle couldn't pretend much longer. She was fighting a losing battle. Her body knew what she wanted even if her mind didn't.

'Please, Rafiq. Don't.' Was that a shimmer of tears in her eyes? He reared back, baffled by her distress. 'This isn't a *real* marriage. It's a—a political alliance. A convenience.' Her mouth twisted on the word and something jabbed deep into his chest. He felt her pain like a physical blow.

'*Habibti*, you are many things, but never a convenience.' He stroked the bright hair back from her face and tried to ignore her responsive shiver. His will-power was a fraying thread, liable to snap at the slightest provocation. And the sight of Belle, her lips swollen from his kisses, her eyes huge and beguiling, her body trembling with the need she sought in vain to hide, was almost more than flesh and blood could withstand.

'You are brave and strong and honest and incredibly sexy.'

His voice dropped to a low rumble. 'And you are my wife. What sort of man would leave you to sleep alone on your wedding night?'

'It's not sleep you've got in mind.'

'Exactly right, little one.' He chuckled as he let his hand slowly circle her breast, satisfied as her eyelids drooped and her breath caught. 'We are wed, Belle. This marriage is no sham. It's real.' Gently he squeezed her breast, and she squirmed beneath his touch.

'No!' She shoved his hand aside and tried to wriggle out from beneath him. 'We need to talk.'

He shook his head, beginning to lose patience. 'We have all the time in the world to talk—later. In the meantime I have something much more satisfying in mind.'

'Can't you just *move*?' She pushed at his shoulders till eventually he rolled back onto his side, giving her a little space.

He frowned. This wasn't just wedding night nerves. There was desperation in her eyes.

'Thank you,' she panted, and it was all he could do to keep his gaze fixed on her face rather than the way her breasts heaved.

'I agreed to marry you to help keep the peace in Q'aroum. *Not* so I could become some royal playmate.'

Rafiq's shoulders tightened at the insult. His jaw clenched. He'd given Belle his protection, his name, had bound himself to her. And she had the gall to cheapen that?

'Nevertheless,' he growled, 'our marriage is legitimate.' He paused as anger churned in his gut. 'Under Q'aroumi law I'm entitled to take what I want from you.'

Her cheeks paled to chalk-white, and immediately he cursed his pride for lashing out at her. He couldn't believe he'd threatened her like that.

'Belle,' he whispered, his voice hoarse with guilt. 'Don't look at me like that.' He stroked the silken length of her hair.

'That was unworthy of me. And of you. You must know I'd never hurt you.'

Slowly she nodded, but her eyes avoided his. She swallowed convulsively and his fingers slid across to span the tender flesh of her throat. Down to cover the heavy gem-encrusted necklace, symbol of al Akhtar possession, down to the place where her heart thudded like a drum.

'I'll never take more than you're willing to give me.'

'But I can't…'

His lips were infinitely gentle at the corner of her mouth, on her bottom lip, as he sought to undo the pain he'd caused. He kept his kisses light as he skimmed her smooth cheek, breathed a caress in her ear and returned to coax open her mouth. For a long moment she hesitated, then finally she kissed him back, tentatively at first. He strove to contain his ardour. But soon their kiss grew deeper, slower, languorous with erotic awareness. She shifted her body against his and he caressed her, circling her breasts, skimming her narrow waist, her hips and thighs. Pulling her close.

Her hands were in his hair, sliding through to hold his head as he angled his mouth over hers. He felt the tension hum in her, the way she pushed against him.

She moaned into his mouth and he tasted her need, a sweet, musky flavour on his tongue. His body tightened in anticipation and he fought the urgency that built within him.

Soon now she'd be his. Soon he'd—

'No!' Her hands were between them again, pushing him back, away from her. 'We can't. This isn't right.'

He drew back enough to read the confusion in her eyes.

If ever a woman was sent to try a man's patience…

'I'm sorry, Rafiq. I should never have kissed you back. I didn't mean to lead you on.' Her eyes met his for a moment, then she looked away, her jaw set. 'I didn't expect that you'd ever want…'

'My wife?' What had she thought—that they'd marry and then lead separate lives? Did he *look* like a man with water in his veins instead of good red blood? 'You have a strange notion of marriage, if that's what you thought.'

Heat flared in her throat, her face, and she bit her lip, teeth sinking savagely into her soft flesh. 'Clearly we had different expectations of this…arrangement.'

'This *marriage*, you mean.' Did she have any notion of what she was asking? Of how difficult it was to lie here with her and *not* make love to her?

'It's academic anyway,' she whispered, looking miserably at a point over his shoulder. 'I have my period.'

Rafiq dried the water from his body and flung the towel away. His jaw ached with the tension that thrummed through him and his neck had set rigidly. His lips curved in a humourless smile. At least the long, cold shower had done its job and relieved him of that other stiffness.

He raked his hand through his hair and sighed. The shower had given him time to think. To plan.

Belle was scared. She'd been through so much in a short space of time, and now she needed time to adjust. It had been too much, too soon for her. She was so brave, so ready to face down her fears, that he'd allowed himself to forget how traumatic these weeks had been for her.

Yes, she wanted him. But she wasn't ready to admit that—even to herself. He needed patience.

For he knew exactly what he wanted: Belle. In his arms. In his bed. His body ached for her, and he had every intention of assuaging that pain.

They were married, and he refused to spend his married life in limbo. The situation had to be resolved—soon—before he self-combusted from the rising heat of lust for his wife.

Damn it all! He still couldn't believe she'd rejected him. He knew she wanted him. Had recognised it almost from the first: the desire she tried so hard to hide.

He could seduce her. The way she responded physically left no doubt in his mind that he'd get his own way if he ignored her protests and tempted her into enjoying their mutual physical pleasure. He could persuade her body into accepting his with minimal effort. That much had been clear from this evening's debacle.

Yet he hesitated to push her into intimacy.

He wanted *all* of her. He wanted Belle, mind *and* body. The willing, eager lover he'd fantasised about.

So he'd take this time that had been forced on him and use it wisely. He'd court her, woo her, tempt her. Till she came to him of her own volition. She might deny it with her words, but there was no doubt she would be his. And soon.

He opened the door and saw moonlight spill from the arched window across the floor to the foot of the bed. Immediately his pulse accelerated as he identified the shape of her, lying under the cotton sheet.

He strode to the other side of the bed, stripped back the cover and got in.

Immediately she rolled over, arm clamped tight over the sheet, as if the fine cotton was some impenetrable barrier between them.

'You can't sleep here,' she hissed.

Rafiq pulled the sheet up to his waist in deference to her modesty—he hadn't missed her quick, startled glance at his naked body. How could he have, when he'd felt it like a searing touch on his bare flesh?

'We're married, Belle. Remember? Where else would a man sleep but with his wife?'

'But—'

'Our marriage is real, *habibti*, never doubt it. I am your husband and I will sleep with you. Tonight and every night.'

Her indrawn breath was loud in the silence that grew between them, but she didn't say anything.

Satisfied he'd made his point, Rafiq settled his head on the pillow, turning to face her.

Immediately she rolled away, towards the far edge of the bed.

He pursed his lips, holding back the oath that surged up. She was stubborn, but she would learn. And, he decided with a smile of anticipation, he was looking forward to educating her.

Hadn't his grandfather instilled in him the value of patience, as well as the ability to harness his instinct to act decisively at the opportune moment? Belle was a challenge unlike any he'd ever tackled. But he knew already the outcome of this battle of wills. Victory would be so sweet. For both of them.

Rafiq reached out under the sheet till he found her. His fingers touched warm silk at her waist, silk that rose and fell with her unsteady breathing.

He had to remember how overwhelming this was for her. First the kidnap. Then the cyclone. The sudden engagement and then a royal wedding with all the pomp and splendour that made it worlds apart from anything she'd ever experienced before. And all this far from home, without the support of her family.

No wonder she was distraught. Confused.

'Shh, *habibti*,' he murmured, and slid forward till his body curved behind hers. Tension hummed through her and he let his arm drop casually across her waist, pulling her unresisting form close against him. 'It's going to be all right. Just relax and go to sleep.'

Her soft hair tickled his mouth. He could feel the gallop of her pulse, hear her ragged, shallow breathing. Beneath the smooth, inviting slide of her nightdress the warm, ripe feminine curves of her body enticed him, bringing him to instant aroused readiness. If he moved his arm just a couple of centimetres he'd be able to stroke her breasts. He was rock-hard with wanting her, shaking with the effort of restraint.

Neither moved. Neither spoke.

Eventually, much, much later, he heard her sigh, felt her body slump into unconsciousness against him. And still he stared over her shoulder into the moonlight, tracing its course across the floor, till eventually it faded, obliterated by the rosy glow of dawn.

Belle woke slowly, her mind fogged by wisps of a delicious dream. A dream where Rafiq held her close and vowed he'd never let her go.

She squeezed her eyes shut tighter, unwilling to wake and lose that fantastic sense of wellbeing just yet. It warmed her still, cocooned her in a glow of delight. She burrowed down into the bed. Just a little longer.

But waking was inevitable, especially when she stretched her leg and found it sliding not across a pure cotton sheet, but along the hair-roughened length of a very hard, very solid and masculine thigh. Her heartbeat revved up and her eyes snapped open.

Warm flesh lay beneath her cheek, and her palm spanned a couple of bare ribs. She blinked. In the night she must have moved. She was spread across Rafiq like a blanket, one leg hitched up over his, her body sprawled as if she couldn't get close enough to him. Only the thin silk of her nightgown lay between them, and she could attest to the fact that it was no barrier at all. Already her body was alert with the possibilities inherent in this position. The silk had rucked up so that her legs were bare, tangled with his. The scent of him was enticing, inviting her to imagine all sorts of things she had no business even to consider.

Already her heart thudded and her breathing shallowed.

Waking up in bed with Rafiq was so—tantalising. So exciting. She wanted to smooth her hand over his firm flesh, learn the shape and texture of his big, relaxed body for herself. Wake him with a kiss and then spend the morning discovering what it was like to be loved by such a man. She suspected it would be wonderful. Stupendous. Addictive.

And therein lay the problem.

She'd built up too many fantasies about him already. He'd figured as rescuer, protector, noble leader making sacrifices for his people. He was imbued with the qualities of loyalty and a profound sense of responsibility that she'd always sought in a man and never found.

The qualities her father had so patently lacked.

Rafiq was honest, direct, worthy of respect. He was a man she knew she could *trust*.

And none of that did justice to the exhilaration she felt when he was near. He wasn't just a pattern card of virtue. He sizzled with sex appeal; he stalked her imagination as a bold pirate, a seductive sheikh whose hooded bedroom eyes promised pleasure beyond anything she'd known.

He'd got right under her guard, bypassed all her defences, her common sense and her caution. He confused her and threatened her ability to think clearly. And now she had a sinking feeling in the pit of her stomach that it was more than infatuation she felt for him. Much more.

She bit her lip and tried to marshal her thoughts.

Why had she been so scared to learn he desired her? Why couldn't she agree to find mutual pleasure in this situation for as long as the marriage lasted?

She'd been astounded to learn he wanted her. He'd kept that hidden so completely that his passion last night had stunned her.

But it wasn't surprise that made her baulk. Or even the fact that she'd never pursued sex for its own sake. It was the innate knowledge that she'd be giving far more than her body into his keeping. That when she left, as she would have to when this situation was finally sorted out, she was in danger of leaving part of herself behind.

Her heart.

Dry-mouthed, Belle faced the truth. She *wanted* Rafiq to make love to her. But she wanted much more. She wanted him to *love* her. She'd stumbled blindly into an untenable situation. If she let him get any closer to her, she might lose her heart to him.

'You're awake, Belle?' His deep voice rumbled softly beneath her ear, making her jump guiltily.

Her head swung up and she met his gaze, glinting with an emotion she couldn't read. Hastily she propped herself up, away from him, shifting back to her side of the bed.

'I'm sorry for crowding you. I didn't mean to—'

'Shh.' His palm covered her mouth and she inhaled the spicy aroma of his skin. Something twisted inside her at his touch.

'No need for apologies, Belle.' He slid his hand away from her mouth slowly, dragging her bottom lip down with his thumb. Then he stroked his fingers down her throat, lightly caressing and oh-so-erotic. The green of his eyes sparked brighter, but his face looked grim.

'I like having you against me while you sleep.' He dropped his hand. 'But since you're awake it's time to move. We should get ready.' He turned to his side of the bed and flung back the sheet.

He was naked, and Belle felt her eyes widen as she caught a glimpse of his massive erection. If her leg had been just a fraction higher as she lay across him...

No, don't go there.

She watched him walk away across the massive room to the *en-suite* bathroom. The morning sun gilded him, glancing off his muscular back and the taut curve of his buttocks. He didn't hurry, but strolled as if he felt no embarrassment being seen naked. Suddenly she felt guilty, devouring him with her eyes.

'Ready for what?' Her voice was a strangled whisper.

He paused in the doorway and turned to meet her gaze over his shoulder. Even from this distance she didn't trust the look in his eyes.

'To go on our honeymoon, of course.'

CHAPTER NINE

'ARE you sure about this?' Belle couldn't prevent the quiver in her voice as she looked down at Rafiq.

'Positive,' he responded, his smile a flash of pure white in his bronzed face. 'You're not scared, are you?'

'No,' she said. But she felt clumsy and uncoordinated, as if she was about to make a fool of herself. And when he grinned up at her like that, with the sun dancing in his eyes, she couldn't breathe properly, much less control a sailboard that seemed to have a mind of its own.

'Would you like me to get up there with you?' His voice deepened a fraction, enough to send a skitter of excitement through her. But his expression remained bland. 'I could stand behind you and guide it.'

Belle shook her head vehemently. He had to be kidding. If he got up here she'd have no choice but to submit to his touch as his arms curved round her and his body pressed close. Like yesterday, when he'd introduced her to archery.

She shut her eyes at the memory. It had taken all her resolve not to break from his hold when she'd felt his warm breath caress her cheek. And when his hard body had encompassed her, arms wrapped around hers, she'd felt weak, the weakness of desire, as he'd murmured instructions in her ear and helped her fit the arrow to the bow. She'd been trembling by the time she finally got an arrow into the target and he'd stepped away.

On a sailboard they'd be even closer. Moving as one. The idea sent a rush of blood to flood her face.

'Belle. Look out!'

But it was too late. She felt the swell of the wave and lunged forward to keep her balance, then overcompensated. She fell back into the water, laughing despite herself. Fifth time unlucky. She obviously had no natural talent for sailboarding.

But her smile vanished as strong arms closed about her, holding her head up above the wave.

'You can let me go,' she whispered, her voice strangely hoarse as she opened her eyes to meet his sea-green gaze so close. His eyes burned with an inner fire. His grin disappeared and there was a closed intensity to his expression that caught her breath. Something heavy pulsed between them, a voiceless communication she'd prefer to ignore, even as her hands settled on his wide shoulders.

'Of course.' He nodded and released her, reaching out instead for the board. She found her feet on the sandy bottom and drew a deep breath.

Nothing had happened. Except for the roiling surge of anticipation deep in her belly when he looked at her like that. As if he saw nothing else but her.

'Perhaps you've had enough? Would you like to go in to shore?' His face was devoid of all emotion. So he'd felt it too—the zap of immediate awareness between them when their bodies collided. Belle had learned a little about her husband in this past week. Including the fact that he kept that particularly wooden expression for use when he wanted to conceal his thoughts.

For the sake of her own peace of mind, she told herself firmly that she had no interest in the thoughts he concealed.

'No.' She shook her head and reached out for the board. 'I'm not ready to be beaten by it just yet.'

Again that grin that transformed his face to breathtaking. 'How did I know you'd say that?'

Despite her caution, Belle felt an answering grin tug at her mouth. Rafiq had come to know her over the past days too: enough to know that she hated being beaten.

'An educated guess?' she said, as she reached out for the board and hoisted herself up.

He didn't answer, just held it steady as she found her footing and reached over to lift the sail from the water. A small wave rolled in, but she kept her balance and slowly hauled the sail up. For a long moment, or two, she was poised, her body a counterweight to the dripping sail. Then, just as she felt she might overbalance, the wind caught the sail and the board moved.

'Shift your weight back,' Rafiq called. But she was already doing it, instinctively finding the right angle to balance the sail. As she did the wind picked up a little and the board shot forward.

She was windsurfing! Gingerly she adjusted her hold. Then the wind was rushing by, and she had to concentrate on standing firm as the board skimmed the waves.

Rafiq was right. It was wonderful, this feeling of power and freedom. Just her and the sea. How had she spent so long living by the ocean and never found time to try sailboarding? Probably the same way she hadn't been on a date in two years—too busy with work.

A large wave caught her suddenly, and wrecked her delicate balance. She felt it go, but couldn't do a thing about it. In slow motion, it seemed, she tipped over into the warm azure water.

She flicked the hair from her eyes as she surfaced. 'Did you see that?' She turned to call out to Rafiq, only to find him a couple of strokes away, swimming towards her.

'I saw,' he said as he stood up. The water was shallower here.

It wasn't just his shoulders that emerged from the sea, but the wide, muscled expanse of his chest. Belle's eyes dropped to his burnished skin, to the sprinkling of dark hair across his chest. It narrowed, she knew, arrowing down towards his slim waist, and lower.

She knew because she saw him morning and night, gloriously naked as he shared his bed with her. And every time it became more difficult not to reach out and touch him. To trace that fine line of hair, to massage the strong muscles, to investigate that gleaming skin.

He was temptation personified. Just the thought of—

'Belle, are you all right?'

She looked up into his face and instantly turned away, afraid of what she might see there. And of what he'd read in her eyes. 'Of course.' She tried to inject enthusiasm into her voice. 'It was great. Just like you said.' She reached out for the board at the same time he did. His hand settled beside hers—large and strong and sinewy compared to hers. Just as his body was larger, harder...

Hell! She had to stop thinking like this. It was driving her crazy.

'Would you like another try?'

'No, thanks. I've had enough for one day. Let's go in.'

'As you wish.' There was no inflection in his tone, and Belle wondered what was going through his mind. Had he guessed that she'd been thinking about the two of them together? She bit her lip as she headed in to the beach. She hoped she wasn't as transparent as she felt.

The problem was that they'd spent all this week together, ostensibly honeymooning at a small fortress-cum-hunting lodge on the isolated north coast. Rafiq had assured her that a honeymoon was expected, and it seemed safer to go through with the charade than invite gossip.

But spending this time with him had only reinforced those

feelings she'd tried to ignore. She'd discovered another side to him. A carefree, fun-loving man who revelled in simple joys like morning horse-rides on the beach and snorkelling at a nearby coral reef. And she'd learned that his smile was just as devastating as his smouldering sensuality when he'd kissed her days ago.

How long ago that seemed.

She sighed and trudged ashore, one hand on the sailboard between them. She couldn't really be wishing he'd kiss her again, could she? She'd be mad if she did. Yet more and more she felt her resolve slipping.

How was she to keep a safe distance between them when he was such good company?

He'd even taken the time to introduce her to Arabic. He'd been giving her impromptu language lessons, saying it would give her confidence. The trouble was she was so busy watching his lips form the sounds, listening to the evocative words that spilled like honey from his mouth, that she couldn't concentrate on their meaning. He must think her the world's worst linguist.

They reached the shore and Rafiq stowed the sailboard in the boatshed. Belle averted her gaze, concentrating on the play of afternoon light across the water, rather than the fluid grace and strength of Rafiq's well-toned body.

'You miss your work?' His voice came, rich and deep, from just behind her. 'Would you rather be out there now on your dive-boat?' There was an edge to his voice that she couldn't identify. This was no idle question.

'Not at all. I was just enjoying the view.' And, amazingly, it was the truth. She'd worked incessantly to build her career in a difficult field, devoting long hours and rarely finding time for holidays.

But this time with Rafiq had been special, despite the difficulties. Despite the tension that paralysed her when he climbed into bed beside her, or when she caught one of his intense looks as he watched her. The week had been fun, exhilarating, the perfect antidote to the stress she'd endured. Rafiq had respected her wishes and not forced himself on her. More than that, he'd given her the experience of a lifetime. She'd never felt so cherished.

She swung round and looked up into his still, brooding face. 'Thank you, Rafiq. I can't remember the last time I enjoyed myself so much. This has been a wonderful holiday.'

The corners of his lips curved up in a slow smile that deepened the grooves beside his mouth and sent a shimmer of longing through her. 'It is entirely my pleasure, Belle. After all, a honeymoon should be noteworthy.'

She opened her mouth to argue that this wasn't *really* a honeymoon, just a pretend one. But what was the point?

'And I'm pleased to hear you're not pining to return just yet to your ancient trading ship.' He lifted a huge beach towel from the bench beside the boathouse and wrapped it round her shoulders, enveloping her in plush cotton and a look of approval that heated her all the way to her toes.

'When we go back to the capital I'd like very much if you'd show me the wreck site. I'd planned to visit earlier and see what progress the team had made.'

She tilted her head to one side, assessing. 'You're that interested?' A lot of people found marine archaeology boring unless it involved bringing up gold. Ancient pottery shards and stone anchors rarely caught the public's imagination.

'Of course. It's part of our history. And besides, it's important to you, Belle. It's only natural I should seek to learn about it.'

Because I'm your husband. He didn't say it, but Belle felt the weight of his meaning heavy in the air between them. It set the hairs on her neck on end.

'How long before the new expedition member arrives?' he asked as he turned away to reach for his towel. 'I don't want you diving alone.'

'I never dive alone,' she said. And then she stopped, her jaw gaping as his words sank in.

'You don't *mind* the idea of me going back to work?'

He swung round and met her gaze with raised eyebrows. 'You're a marine archaeologist, and a dedicated one from what I've discovered. How could I mind?'

'But as your…wife—' she stumbled on the word '—I thought—'

'That I'd take a medieval view of a woman's role?' His lips stretched in that devastating smile that made her insides melt. 'Now, that would be interesting option: keeping you secreted in my harem. Seeing no men but me. Awaiting my pleasure.'

A blush of fierce heat scorched Belle's cheeks as she read the amusement in his eyes. And the flicker of something else— something that told her the idea appealed to him, just as it did to some tiny, primitive part of her subconscious. She took a half-step back, away from him.

'I'm afraid not, little one. Unless you'd like to give up your career and devote yourself entirely to me?' He paused while she tried to unstick her tongue from the roof of her mouth. His tone told her he was joking. Wasn't he?

'No?' He reached out and took her elbow in his hand, turning her towards the steps that led up the cliff to the lodge. 'What a shame. But it's as I expected. My own mother was a qualified paediatrician when my parents wed. She continued to run clinics all through their marriage.'

'I didn't know.' She *had* assumed that she'd have a battle on her hands when the time came to return to work.

'How could you?' They reached the bottom of the steps and he gestured for her to go first. 'Don't worry, Belle, you'll be able to work—though perhaps not the same hours you were devoting to the project in the past.'

This was one huge weight lifted off her shoulders. She was

still in a bind, tied by a formal marriage contract for the foreseeable future. But at least she'd be able to pursue her career. She'd feared she'd have to opt out of the expedition she'd strived so hard to join.

Impulsively she stopped and swung round. Rafiq was right behind her, his eyes almost level as he stood on the step below hers.

'Thank you, Rafiq. That means a lot to me.' She wanted to hug him, to thank him properly for being so reasonable.

'I'm gratified to have made you happy, Belle.' His voice was deep and soft, caressing. His gaze held hers and she sucked in a shaky breath. 'It is a matter of great importance to me that you are content.'

Belle stared, mesmerised by those gleaming eyes. His breath hazed her skin. His body, so close, was an invitation to sensual pleasure she could barely ignore. But, more than that, she felt a glow of happiness, knowing he respected her, cared for her enough to put her needs first. He'd done it time and again. By accepting her insistence on a platonic relationship. By accommodating her need to work. By going out of his way to make this strange new world as wife of the Sheikh a delight rather than a burden.

Her husband really was the most extraordinary man.

Was it any wonder she'd finally done the unthinkable? She'd fallen in love with him.

Belle woke next morning to the pearly light of dawn and for the first time found herself alone in the bed.

It was unsettling.

She'd become used to the luxury of Rafiq's body warming hers when she woke. To the forbidden thrill of delight his touch always evoked.

They shared an enormous bed Rafiq had told her was generations old. Its carvings were so dark and worn that she couldn't make them out. But she suspected the figures cavorting on the headboard were mermaids. Each night she'd lain here, her heart in her mouth, as she watched him from beneath her lashes. And when he took her in his arms she was torn between exultation and dread. She longed for his lovemaking, yet feared the consequences. She loved him but knew this marriage wasn't for ever.

How could she admit her love, act upon it, and then turn away from him when the time came?

And how could she even consider giving herself to a man who, despite his fine qualities, would never reciprocate her feelings? She had no doubt his own choice of partner would be someone glamorous and gorgeous, born to wealth and power, someone who would fit into the role of royal princess as she never could.

Yet every day she woke to find her legs tangled with his, the hot, musky scent of him enticing, his erection blatant and tempting against her. And each morning her resolve to keep her distance weakened further.

His eyes were unfathomable. He spent so much time just watching her, she wondered what he saw.

'There you are, Belle.' She swung round as he entered the room and, as usual, her heart skipped faster.

He wore trousers and boots with a long-sleeved white shirt open at the neck to reveal his sun-bronzed throat. His hair was pulled back from his face and he was smiling. The force of it sizzled up her spine.

'Where have you been?'

'You missed me?' he asked as he strode across to the bed. He reached for her hand and lifted it to his mouth, his gaze locked with hers. Slowly he kissed her hand, sending a shaft of pure heat arcing through her body. He turned her hand over and kissed her palm. This time she shivered, feeling the inevitable slow burn in the pit of her belly ignite into blazing fire.

She'd never get used to the sheer seductive power of those

caresses. 'Just wondered where you were,' she said shakily, pulling her hand away.

'A video conference. And I had a surprise to prepare.' He cast a lingering glance over her as she lay, covered by the sheet. 'You'll need a long-sleeved shirt and a hat,' he said. 'It'll be blazing hot in the desert later.'

'The desert?'

He nodded. 'I'm taking you on a picnic.'

Two hours later, mounted on the most placid of the purebred Arab horses in the stables, Belle reined in and stared at the oasis in the gully below. A tiny Garden of Eden in the midst of sand dunes. Palm trees towered over smaller trees and shrubs. She caught the glint of water in the sunlight and the sound of birds rose from the greenery.

'Like it?' Rafiq asked.

'It's lovely.' She'd always lived on the coast, and the stark beauty of the desert had been a surprise. With Rafiq at her side, pointing out rock forms, animal tracks, the way the wind sculpted the dunes, the graceful shadow of a hunting falcon, she'd enjoyed every minute of the ride.

'Come on,' he urged.

She nodded. 'You start down,' she said. 'I'll follow.'

She loved watching him ride, with the easy grace of a born horseman. As much at home in the saddle as he'd been on his yacht a few days ago. With his headscarf protecting him from the sun, the bright light illuminating his commanding profile and the breeze plastering his shirt against his chest, she couldn't drag her gaze away.

She swallowed hard, reminding herself that this was no romantic fantasy. But she couldn't prevent the tingle of awareness that heightened her senses at the sight of him: strong and vital, utterly spellbinding with his aura of raw, masculine power.

And he's yours. All you have to do is reach out to him, whispered the voice of temptation.

She battled that demon ceaselessly, desperate to control the feelings that threatened to consume her: the admiration, the desire. She lusted for him so badly he must read it in the very scent of her skin, the taut awareness of her body, attuned as it was to his every move.

Had he guessed that, despite her rearguard manoeuvres to remain aloof, she'd lost her heart? That his wife in this arranged marriage had fallen in love with him?

She drew in a shuddering breath and took the track down to the wadi, aware of his piercing gaze as he waited.

It still shocked her, the suddenness and completeness of her love for him. The irrevocability of it. How could her world centre on him alone?

He was a man of integrity, but they were married, so, from his viewpoint, he had rights to her body. Why not find mutual pleasure?

Yet she was terrified that if they became physically intimate her feelings would enslave her to someone who, however admirable, didn't love her.

'Belle?'

She looked into his enticing green gaze, read the welcome, the answering desire in his face, and felt her self-control splinter. How could she resist him?

'Come,' he said. 'I have a surprise for you.'

Something danced in his eyes—amusement? Anticipation? Her pulse thrummed faster.

The horses picked their way down the slope to water that reflected the brilliant blue of the sky. There were a couple of long pools running through the centre of the tiny valley, the heart of its green burgeoning life.

Rafiq's hands closed round her waist and he lifted her down to stand toe to toe with him. Heat spread from his encompassing grip, and her breath caught at the sensation of his leashed power. His encircling hands made her feel small and vulnerable. The blaze of fire in his eyes told her he felt it too, the need, the suspense.

Desire was a searing curl of tension winding tight in her womb. Coiling harder and faster, till her breathing constricted and her breasts peaked and throbbed.

His breath fanned her. She saw the rapid pulse at the base of his neck and the urge to kiss that spot, taste his skin with her tongue, made her sway in his hold.

Abruptly he let her go and stepped away. Something—disappointment—was a hard knot in her stomach.

'Belle,' he said, and his tone made her shiver. His expression was taut as his gaze skimmed over her. It was no consolation to know he found this difficult too. Her whole body quivered from the pounding tension that grew and circled still inside her.

'Come,' he said, his voice low. He took her hand and drew her forward. 'I think you'll like it.'

Slowly she followed him, looking anywhere but at him. Pretending she didn't feel the awareness that pulsed between them through their linked hands.

They rounded a clump of thorn bushes and she saw it. A traditional nomad's tent set beneath a grove of tall date palms. And in front of it a slim ribbon of rippling water that flowed and widened into another waterhole. She gasped in amazement and delight at the scene. At this side of the tent was an opening, raised like an awning to reveal an interior luxuriant with rugs in dark jewel colours.

'How did you do this?' she asked, eyes fixed on the enchanting sight. With its burnished hanging lamp at the entrance and the scatter of cushions she could make out at the rear of the tent, it looked like something out of an old storybook. A place Scheherazade could have described.

His hand squeezed hers. 'You approve?'

'I love it.' She smiled up at him and caught a glimpse of some expression, quickly hidden, in his bright scrutiny. 'But how is it here? When did you—?'

'There was a security sweep of the area by helicopter a little earlier. They brought out a few supplies for our picnic on their way.' He smiled. 'If ever we were in the desert overnight we'd use this tent, my grandfather and I. I felt sure you'd appreciate it.'

A few supplies. Belle stared at the vision before her and stifled a laugh. Where she came from a picnic meant a hamper and an old blanket.

'It's wonderful. Thank you, Rafiq.'

'My pleasure, Belle.' His voice had deepened to a note that sent a tremor of response through her. His eyes met hers and her breath snagged.

'Let's clean up a little.' He led her to the water.

'The horses—'

'They'll be fine,' he said as he leaned to scoop water over his face and hands. 'They won't stray.'

The water was surprisingly cool against her heated skin, and she let it dribble down her collarbone, revelling in the refreshing trails that ran under the loose cotton of her shirt. She washed her dusty hands and turned to find Rafiq watching her. That was nothing new. He did that all the time, quietly observing and giving nothing away.

But this time there was something in his look that unnerved her. Send the blood rushing to her face.

He held out his hand and led her into the tent.

Her immediate impression was of dim coolness after the hot, bright desert sun. Her second was of its sheer luxury. There were patterned rugs on the walls, insulation against the heat. Overlapping carpets covered every inch of the floor, and if she'd been alone she'd have thrown herself down immediately on the inviting pile of huge cushions. There were a couple of low, polished brass tables and, incongruously, a huge portable icebox in one corner.

She followed Rafiq's example and took off her shoes, immediately grateful when she felt the caress of finely woven silk beneath her feet. She stared. Each of these carpets must be worth a fortune.

'Come. Make yourself comfortable while I get you a drink.' Rafiq gestured to the cushions.

She padded across the rugs, feeling with every step as if she strayed further from the reality of her modern world into a shadowed place where time slowed to the pace of a heartbeat. The aroma of sandalwood scented the air, and even the shadows were painted with rainbow hues from the profusion of exquisite fabrics.

'It's amazing,' she whispered as she subsided onto a huge brocade pillow, grateful for its soft comfort after the hard saddle. 'I've never seen anything like it.'

'I'm honoured that you approve.' His deep voice came from above her, and he bent to press iced juice into her hand. Even the glass was decorated with gold filigree.

'Thank you,' she whispered, her throat suddenly dry as she stared into his hooded gaze. His face was unreadable, but his lips curved into a smoky half-smile that sent her pulse into crazy overdrive.

She took refuge in the act of sipping her drink, lowering her gaze from his. The juice was tart and sweet, unlike anything she'd ever tasted.

'It's a traditional mixture,' he said. 'Pomegranate and melon, with mint and a few other things.'

'It's delicious—thank you.' The words sounded stilted, as if this polite, meaningless conversation barely masked the brooding, intense silence between them. A silence thick with other messages. All unspoken. All dangerous.

'This morning's been lovely,' she said quickly, as he seated himself beside her with the loose-limbed suppleness that made his every movement a study in masculine grace. 'I wouldn't have thought there'd be so much water here—not when we're surrounded by desert,' she babbled, needing to keep the conversation going.

'It's good swimming here too. The water's invigorating.' His words were bland but his look seared. Immediately she envisaged them both, naked in the water, and her temperature soared as blood suffused her whole body. She gulped down the rest of her juice and looked round for somewhere to put the glass.

'Here,' he said, taking it from her and stretching across to place it on a nearby low table.

Too late Belle realised her mistake. Now she had nothing to keep her hands occupied. And more than ever it seemed imperative to have something to concentrate on.

Other than Rafiq.

'Thanks,' she murmured. 'But I didn't come prepared for swimming.'

'As you wish,' he said, inclining his head, then letting the silence lengthen. He put his glass down beside hers and leaned back, propped on one elbow, to watch her. 'This is your first trip here. We will do whatever pleases you.'

Whatever pleases me... Belle scanned his handsome face and barely concealed the quiver of pure need that seared through her. This close to him she breathed in the unique, seductive scent that was simply Rafiq. Every night it tantalised her as she lay against him, frozen into immobility by the fear that a single unguarded movement might shatter the brittle barrier of her self-control.

She wanted him so much.

'Belle?' His deep, sultry voice was temptation. He took her hand, laid it across his palm and stroked the sensitive skin between thumb and forefinger till her nerves prickled. Her breath caught as she stared at him, mesmerised by the raw passion in his gaze.

'You only have to ask for anything you want,' he whispered.

'I want…' She heaved a sigh as she slammed common sense down on the unspoken need that consumed her. She couldn't tell him what she really wanted.

But his gaze had dropped to her breasts, drawn by her uneven breathing. Immediately her breasts felt fuller, uncomfortable against the restraint of her bra, her nipples pebbling in instant response to the banked fire of his unblinking gaze. A shaft of white-hot need speared down through her, igniting the core of her desire.

'You want?' He raised his eyes to hers and she was lost. Defeated by the ardour she saw there.

'I want…you to kiss me,' she whispered unsteadily.

He raised her hand to his mouth and kissed the back of it, his fiery gaze holding her transfixed. Then slowly he turned it over and pressed an open-mouthed kiss on her palm. This time she felt the hot caress of his tongue on the pleasure point at the centre of her hand, and squeezed her eyes shut as the tremor of delight intensified into shudders of fervent need.

'Is that all you want?' he murmured against her skin, pressing kisses along each of her fingers.

Belle felt her careful barriers collapse and shatter under the sensual onslaught of Rafiq's intense caresses and her own longing.

'I want…' She hissed in a sharp breath as his teeth grazed the heel of her hand and she felt the hot, moist proof of her desire pool between her legs.

She curled her fingers tight round his and opened her eyes. He was so close, watching her with a smouldering intensity that snatched her breath away.

When she could summon the words she whispered, 'I want you to make love to me.'

CHAPTER TEN

HER heavy-lidded eyes darkened, her skin flushed with passion, her words echoed in the waiting stillness between them. And Rafiq knew he'd won.

The surge of triumphant elation that flooded his veins was so intense, so overpowering, that he froze, battling with all his strength to retain a semblance of composure. He felt it slam through him like a runaway train—the need to have her, take her, stamp his ownership on her in the most primitive and undeniable way.

He saw the unguarded longing in her eyes, smelled the unmistakable sweet scent of feminine desire, felt the dampening of her petal-soft skin, and knew that she wanted him the way he wanted her. Now. Immediately. No preliminaries, no debate. Just the need to lose themselves in the mindless, dazzling passion that raged like a spiralling desert storm between them.

It would be superb. It would be cataclysmic.

It would be over almost before it had begun.

She deserved better than that. Much better.

He dragged in a breath, laden with the heady scent of her, and yielded to the impulse to taste her again, this time laving her palm. He didn't trust himself to take her mouth, not yet.

Even now, just knowing she was his, he was so hard, so ready, that a single unguarded movement could be catastrophic.

Her lids fluttered closed and she sighed. But she wasn't content to wait for his lovemaking. She dragged her hand from his and reached for him, leaning forward to slip both arms over his shoulders and round his neck.

'Rafiq,' she murmured in a voice of pure seduction. Her lips were parted, waiting, her body taut against his.

He'd been right, he thought grimly. Now that her formidable reserve had been breached and her passion unleashed, Belle had transformed into a *houri*, the most seductively dangerous woman known to mankind. Everything about her promised a heaven of earthly pleasures. The way she breathed his name with such longing almost betrayed him into surrendering to the temptation of instant gratification. Without conscious thought he clamped his hands on her waist. He felt her writhe beneath his hold, circling her hips in age-old invitation. One more move and she'd find her trousers pushed down to her knees and him inside her, throbbing his release.

'Belle,' he groaned. The very thought of sinking into her waiting warmth was too dangerous. It brought him to the brink of sanity.

Gritting his teeth, ignoring the internal howl of outrage, the biting need to take her instantly, he slid his hands away, shifted his body and found his footing. Before she could object he scooped her up against him, then stood with her cradled in his arms. He knew his hold was too tight, pressing hard into her flesh. But he was functioning on raw instinct, the voice of his better judgement barely audible over the blood-rush of primitive emotions.

Her eyes opened wide, but she didn't look around as he strode to the far corner of the tent, kicking cushions out from underfoot. Her eyes were fixed on his, their expression an indefinable mix of excitement, blazing heat and…trepidation?

Could it be? Fear, from his indomitable Belle?

It brought him up short at the edge of the vast sleeping platform. But now, try as he might, he could no longer read the emotions in her eyes. Had that anxiety been real or an illusion?

It was too late, he realised as he lowered her to the silken coverlet. Nothing could stop them becoming one. But that flash of doubt was enough to take the edge off his rapacious need to strip her clothes away and take her without further preliminaries. It restored just a fraction of his sense of responsibility.

'You asked me to make love to you, *habibti*,' he murmured in a voice that sounded thick and strange to his ears. 'Just relax,' he said, as he skimmed his hands down her body, then back up to the buttons of her loose cotton shirt.

Relax! Belle stared into his strong, stern face and wondered if he realised how laughable, how impossible, was his command.

Each nerve in her body throbbed with unfulfilled desire, with days of wanting this man till her body screamed its need every time he touched her. Did he have any idea how desperate she was for this? For his embrace? His kiss? His lovemaking?

His hands worked deftly at the buttons of her shirt, his touch deliberate, calm, slow. She bit into her bottom lip, trying to court the patience to lie passive beneath his ministrations, but it was impossible. She reached out for his shirt, caught the fine lawn in trembling fingers and fumbled at the first button.

'No!' His voice was a muted roar of disapproval and she blinked.

'No, *habibti*. Do not touch. Not yet.' His fingers clamped around her wrists and dragged them away from him. She looked into his brilliant eyes and felt the burn of raw desire in his stare. It was incendiary, igniting the flames of secret need within her.

How could he ask her not to touch him? It was unthinkable. She had opened her mouth to object when he put one arm round her, lifting her up a fraction so he could slide her shirt from her shoulders and toss it away. Then her loosened bra disappeared too.

He settled her back on the bed, and this time she lay still, pinioned by the hot, possessive light in his eyes. Her breasts peaked shamelessly under his scrutiny, and a flood of searing heat scorched every inch of her skin.

'You are even more beautiful than I expected,' he whispered as he stroked a light touch across first one breast than the other. Her breath hitched in her chest at the incredible sensuality of that barely-there caress. Then she gasped as his touch slowed, stilled, sharpened, his fingers tugging on her nipple so that darts of luscious sensation speared down to her very core.

'Rafiq! Please.' She squirmed beneath him.

'Do I hurt you, Belle?' Already his touch had altered, his palm slipping flat across her skin.

'No, you don't hurt. I just…'

Her words died as she registered his predatory smile. His head lowered till his lips caressed her with tiny kisses. When he moved to suckle at her breast she couldn't contain the jolt of delight that made her stiffen beneath him. It was so much, so wonderful. But not enough. She wrapped her arms round his shoulders, tilted her hips towards him. He was propped beside and above her and she needed his weight on her now.

Her hands grew urgent as his teased and pleasured her. Did he have any idea what sort of torture this was?

Oh, yes, she decided, remembering the glint of powerful knowledge in his eyes. He knew and revelled in her need for him.

Here she was, helpless and yearning, wild for his touch, laying her heart as well as her body open for him, just as she'd feared she would if she lost the strength to resist him. But somehow, now it had happened, now she had given in to her feelings, she couldn't regret it. Not when he was taking her to paradise. She'd craved him incessantly and it had been only fear holding her back. A fear he had banished with a single touch.

She slid her hands down to his shirt and managed to slip a couple of buttons undone, to feel the raw heat of his bare flesh against her fingers before he moved again.

'Soon,' he said, and she saw the slumberous promise in his eyes. 'But not yet.'

She almost cried out her protest, but then he was undoing her trousers with quick, decisive movements, stripping the last of her clothes away so she lay naked and trembling before him.

There was a flash of something fierce and untamed in his face as he surveyed her, spread out before him like some waiting harem slave. His eyes burned and the planes of his face grew more pronounced, as if tension pared his features to their stark, elemental beauty.

In that instant Belle knew fear, and something else, something stronger. Triumph. His need for her was blatant—in the rigid control she read in his face and in the taut, dangerous lines of his broad shoulders and clenched fists.

And suddenly she didn't feel vulnerable any more. Lying naked before him wasn't embarrassing or demeaning. It was liberating, intoxicating. The balance of power between them had shifted, and she revelled in the knowledge that he was frozen still with the effort of control. She could seduce as well as be seduced.

'Rafiq,' she whispered, surprised at the throaty, knowing sound of her voice. 'Won't you touch me?'

She watched him swallow down hard. He shuddered. His knuckles whitened.

Belle smiled, confident that in this at least they were equals. He might not love her, but his body craved hers just as badly as hers did his.

Slowly she reached up to the traditional headdress he'd worn for the desert ride. She fumbled, and he lifted a hand to untuck one end of the long piece of linen. She took it from him and smiled, a trembling curve of the lips, as she unwound the scarf. Her eyes locked with his but she could read nothing there now; they were too closely shuttered.

At last the cloth came away in her hands and she let it drop, absorbed instead by the swing of shining black hair that fell about his shoulders. Fleetingly she wondered how it could so enhance his hard masculinity.

Then she dropped her hands to his shirt, swiftly dispensing with the buttons till she'd bared enough to be able to slip her hands in against his firm chest, luxuriating in the heat of his skin against hers, the teasing rasp of his chest hair against her fingers.

Rafiq tore open the rest of the buttons in a single ruthless movement, and she sighed, sliding her hands round his torso and nestling against him. His heartbeat was a thunderous tattoo beneath her ear. His chest rose and fell against her with every deep breath he drew. His scent, hot musk, settled around her, and the silk of his unbound hair caressed her face.

So many sensations. But not enough. She craved more. She needed everything from him.

Her tongue flicked out so she could taste the hot, salty essence of him. She pressed open-mouthed kisses across his pectoral muscle, finding and nuzzling his taut nipple as her hand strayed lower, following the trail of narrowing dark hair that led down his abdomen. From deep inside his chest came a low, thrumming vibration. She felt more than heard the untamed growl as she reached for the fastening on his trousers.

Then, in a surge of powerful movement, she found herself thrust back against the bed, pinioned by his uncompromising weight. He grabbed her hands in one of his and slammed them back, over her head, onto the silk covers.

'Rafiq?' Belle loved the feel of him over her, pushing against her, but the move had startled her.

'You must not touch me.' His voice was a hoarse throb, barely recognisable. His eyes glittered feverishly as he stared down at her.

Not touch him? She frowned. Was this some weird royal protocol she'd breached? She shook her head in confusion.

'Belle—' He stopped and closed his eyes. The only sign of his agitation was the iron-hard tension in his body and the way his chest heaved.

'Belle,' he said again, and she heard raw pain in his deep voice. 'I cannot let you touch me. Not yet. Not if you want to be loved instead of ravaged.'

Excitement pulsed through her, fast and heavy, as she absorbed his words. The idea of being ravaged by him sounded magnificent.

'Rafiq, I— What are you doing?' She stared as he eased her hands lower and dragged the end of his abandoned headscarf across them.

His thumb stroked tenderly along the fading scar on her wrist and he frowned. 'Does it still hurt?'

She shook her head. Her scars had healed well, and soon, she hoped, there'd be no visible sign they'd existed.

He nodded, and carefully looped the soft cotton around both wrists, binding them together.

Belle's jaw dropped. He couldn't mean to…?

Sensing her outraged confusion, he paused and looked down at her. 'Do you trust me, Belle?' The words were softly spoken, but she read the taut stillness in his body as he waited for her response.

For an aching moment the shadow of terror skittered through her, with the memory of her abductors closing rusty manacles around her wrists. But fear dissolved at the sight of Rafiq, the man she loved, painfully tense, his jaw locked in a savage attempt at control, his fingers shaking as he cupped her hands in his.

Did she trust him?

She felt her smile spread slowly, inexorably, across her face as she realised just how completely she trusted him. Despite her denials, she'd given him not only her body, but her heart, her whole self, with their marriage.

'I trust you, Rafiq.'

She saw him shudder in relief. 'Belle.' His thumb brushed her lips, caressed her cheek and throat. She turned her head and pressed a kiss against his palm.

'Please, Rafiq. Love me.'

Something wonderful, bright and exultant, flared in his eyes as they held hers. She felt a burgeoning sense of expectation, and more, of emotional connection.

His mouth lowered to hers in a fleeting, tempting brush of lips and he murmured, 'You honour me, *Belle.*'

Then he shifted his weight and stretched above her, so that her world narrowed to the wall of his chest, centimetres above her, the weight of his legs covering her and the heady scent of him.

There was a gentle tug on her wrists as he drew them back, over her head, and towards the tent pole behind the sleeping platform. For an instant doubt gnawed at her. How had she agreed to something that left her so much at his mercy?

But then Rafiq slid back down her body and her every nerve clamoured for more. His mouth lowered to hers in a slow, lingering kiss that re-ignited her craving for fulfilment. It was the sort of kiss she'd dreamed about, a lover's kiss that touched her heart as much as her physical senses. If she hadn't known it was impossible she'd be tempted to think Rafiq reciprocated her love.

The idea made her head swim. Or perhaps it was the sheer sensual expertise of his kiss.

And as his tongue slid into her mouth, taking possession, he shifted his weight to one side, keeping his muscled thigh across hers. His hand skimmed the sensitive flesh of her neck, her breasts, her waist, brushing to the curve of her hips. She craved his touch, needing so much more than this gentle, gliding caress. She twisted beneath him, only the tie anchoring her hands preventing her from reaching out to pull him closer.

When his hand slid across the juncture of her thighs she felt a jolt of white-hot energy stab through her.

But he didn't break the kiss, simply plunged deeper into her mouth as his fingers brushed across that most sensitive point again, and she jerked beneath him, her whole body humming with expectation. His knee nudged at her legs, parting them, so that when he touched her intimately again she was wide open to his teasing caress.

She moaned, yanked at her bonds, desperate for release. This wasn't what she wanted. She wanted Rafiq. She wanted…

'Rafiq!' Her cry was one of astonished urgency. He lifted his head to watch her as, with one last delicate touch, he sent her soaring into explosive climax. Turbulent, molten heat surged through her as her whole body juddered in the aftershocks of that single, intense, pulsing moment.

And through it all his gaze held hers, watching as she gasped for breath, as her face flooded with heat and her eyes widened in shock.

She should have felt embarrassed, exposed. But the heated intensity in his eyes, the slow, infinitesimal curve of his lips so close to hers held her in thrall.

'You are beautiful, little tigress,' he murmured, and she felt his breath as a caress across her lips. 'So responsive and vibrant.' He ducked his head and nipped at her lower lip with his teeth.

It was as if he'd found a new, untapped erogenous zone. Her response was immediate—a sudden, impossible zap of lightning awareness that stiffened her body and snagged her breath.

'Let me go, Rafiq.' She tried to catch his mouth with hers, but he pulled back just enough that she couldn't reach him. 'Please,' she gasped. 'I need you.'

'And you shall have me, Belle. All in good time.' But instead of reaching up to wrench open the knot binding her hands to the tent pole he moved lower, to suckle at her breast.

Her breath stopped at the sight of him there, one large, tanned hand on her pale skin, thumb teasing her nipple, his lips closing over her other breast. And the feel of him. The moist caress of his mouth, the sensual slide of his hair over her aroused body and the weight of him, all heavy muscle and masculine hardness, centred over her, pushing her down into the bedding.

'Untie me,' she urged through dry lips.

His green eyes glinted with sensual purpose as he took her nipple between his teeth and gently tugged.

'Rafiq!' She was on fire again, aching for more than this teasing. Frantic, she pulled on the cloth tying her hands, but it only seemed to draw tighter with each movement.

'Shh, *habibti*.' His voice was like velvet, brushing across her raw nerves. 'Don't fight it. I'll release you soon, very soon,' he whispered as he pressed a kiss to the sensitive underside of her breast.

But Rafiq's definition of soon was vastly different from hers. Instead of loosing the bonds that kept her from reciprocating his touch, he seemed to revel in his complete freedom to touch, taste, caress her bare body. He had no compunction in using his uncompromising weight and his strength to hold her still beneath him as he investigated every centimetre of her.

Yet it wasn't a clinical survey of her body. Oh, no. It was an erotic voyage of discovery. For Rafiq, as he nuzzled and licked and stroked. And for Belle, as she learned how shockingly responsive she was to him. Never before had she experienced such exquisite sensuality, nor responded so wantonly, so completely to a man. He brought her to trembling ecstasy time and again, giving even as he took such obvious pleasure in her.

And through all the delicious torture of his loving she read the fierce light of possession in his eyes. He was branding her with his touch, searing her senses with the sight and smell and taste of him, till she knew nothing else. Enslaving her body just as, unknowingly, he'd captured her heart.

The tremors were subsiding at last from her limbs, to be replaced with a luscious, weightless feeling. She glowed, lit from within by an incandescent sense of wellbeing. Her eyes drifted shut and she stretched slowly, luxuriously, aware for the first time that Rafiq had moved and she could shift her legs across the soft silk of the coverlet. The cushioned bedding invited slumber, and Belle felt the last of the tension ease from her body as she sank deeper into welcoming oblivion.

Soft, warm darkness. Soothing, slow, caressing heat. She smiled dreamily and shifted into a more comfortable position. It was only as he gripped her hips that Belle realised this was no dream. The heat was Rafiq's, and he had lowered his naked body over hers.

Her eyes popped open, widening as he shifted his weight and she felt the searing length of his erection press down against her belly. He felt impossibly large, frighteningly potent as he pushed forward. Yet her hips rose automatically to meet him, and she felt that tiny spark stir again, deep inside.

Rafiq's gaze locked with hers. He didn't smile, didn't speak. His eyes had a glazed look, as if he focussed inwards. She read iron-hard control in the muscles that strained in his neck and shoulders. And then, with a single, slow, unstoppable movement, he eased down into her till she was pinioned against him.

She risked a deep breath, aware of muscles stretching impossibly to accommodate him, wary of moving. She'd wanted this so badly, wanted Rafiq as she'd never wanted before. And now she wasn't sure this would work. Then he shifted his weight and pulled her legs higher, easing the tension a fraction, sliding even deeper.

His head dipped to graze a kiss along her neck, and she heard his voice, husky and breathless, murmuring words she couldn't understand. The thread of inevitable tension tugged through her as he kissed her, making her squirm. Immediately she felt his responsive quiver of anticipation, and revelled in the sensation.

'Please,' she whispered. 'Please untie me now.'

He didn't seem to have heard her. Instead he rocked gently back, and then forwards again, creating a perfect friction between them.

It shouldn't have been possible, she told herself, but there was no doubting the way her body responded to his magnificent virility. She'd been loved to satiation, beyond endurance, and yet she tingled with growing anticipation at every slow, silent thrust of his body.

Her eyes widened as she felt it again, the scorching flame of desire.

His movements grew faster, his breath against her skin laboured, and she responded, knowing nothing but her love for this man, her need to give him everything. And that shuddering sense of expectation.

And then he was kissing her, and it was the epitome of every romantic fantasy. There was obvious sexuality in that caress, but there was more. She would swear to it. He'd tapped into her very soul with his loving, and now this was far more than the most erotic experience of her life. It was the culmination of all her hopes and dreams. It was the caress of a lover, a soul-mate.

Her hands slid through his glorious hair, gripping the back of his skull so she could give back kiss for breathtaking kiss. His own hands were roving, sliding heavy and possessive over her, before clamping again on her hips as he increased the tempo of their movements. And then she held him in her arms, hands splayed over the febrile heat of his damp skin, feeling the bunching muscles as he pushed them both towards the inevitable fulfilment that awaited.

The moment hovered, just beyond reach, and then, with an abruptness that astounded her, she was caught in a joint conflagration that spiralled far beyond anything that had gone before.

It was only with the hoarse echo of her own name in her ears, with the sudden burden of Rafiq's full weight on her body as he slumped onto her, that she realised how tightly her fingers dug into the spare flesh of his back.

He'd untied her hands, so she could caress him.

She squeezed her eyes tight shut against the absurd tears that flooded her eyes. She had no idea why she was crying. It was ridiculous, appalling. And utterly unstoppable.

CHAPTER ELEVEN

'Shh, *habibti*. Don't cry.' His voice was thick and he wasn't sure she'd heard. He rolled to his side, wrapping his arms around her, then pulled her on top of him as he lay flat on his back. She sprawled bonelessly above him, her shoulder-length hair splayed across his chest, her legs, smooth and supple, tangled with his. Her hot tears spilled onto his skin and he reached up to stroke her back.

His hand slid down the exquisite curve from her shoulder to her narrow waist, and then traced the flare of her hip. It was bewitching, the feel of her fine-grained skin beneath his palm. He couldn't believe how a single touch, an attempt to comfort her, could arouse him again—and so soon.

Yet so it was.

Even after that long, passionate sojourn, learning the secrets of her body, revelling in the trust she gave him so freely, it wasn't enough. The simple graze of flesh against flesh excited him now as if he'd never had the chance to touch her before.

'It's all right,' he murmured against her hair. 'There's nothing to cry about.'

She nuzzled his chest and he felt a sharp pang arrow into him. A pang of pure pleasure, he realised with shock.

'I know,' she mumbled. 'It doesn't make any sense.'

He heard another stifled sob and drew her tight against him, whispering soothing words in his own language, rubbing her shoulder with one hand while his other clamped her close.

He felt like a fraud. To all intents and purposes he was comforting her. Yet inside he was revelling in the knowledge that her tears were nothing more nor less than the aftermath of the sensual journey he'd taken her on. He'd lost count of the times she'd climaxed under his touch. Had known he should give in to her hoarse cries to let her go. But selfishness had driven him on. Selfish pleasure at the unstinting way she responded to each new caress and a wholly self-centred desire to mark his ownership deep in her psyche. To make her so utterly his that there'd be no doubt, ever, in her mind that she belonged to him.

He should have untied her long before. Should have listened to her pleas for release before he tipped her into this emotional state.

He should have. But he wondered if, given the same circumstances again, he'd have the strength to act differently.

She'd been so unstintingly responsive, so much an embodiment of those midnight fantasies that had kept him wakeful every night since he found her. It would have taken far more strength than he possessed to let her be.

He'd tied her hands simply because, if he'd let her touch him again, he wouldn't have been able to restrain himself. He would have exploded as violently as the fireworks on the night of their wedding. And far, far too soon.

Yet honesty made him admit, at least to himself, that he'd found the act of binding her hands, of having her helpless before him, so sexually stimulating that he'd allowed himself free rein. He hadn't been content when she'd shuddered in his arms once, even twice. It was as if he'd grown addicted to her hoarse mews of excitement, to the flare of astonished exhilaration in her eyes as he brought her to peak after peak.

He'd fed his own ego with her unbridled responses under the guise of preparing her for his body. True, he'd wondered if she'd experience discomfort when they came together, given her delicate proportions and his own size. He'd been determined to ease the way. But he'd gone too far. He listened to her subsiding sniffs and knew he'd taken far more from her than he'd given.

'Sleep now, Belle. Just sleep.'

He felt her yawn against his bare chest and clamped down on the realisation of how very much he wanted to feel her lips on his body.

She snuggled into him, her hair teasing his flesh and her weight unconsciously provocative.

Rafiq gritted his teeth as he realised with mirthless humour how he was paying now for his unfettered lust in seducing her so thoroughly. She was sated, exhausted. And here he was, already eager for her again. Yet even a man so acutely tempted as he couldn't in conscience impose himself on her again so soon. She needed rest.

He knew he deserved every bit of this torture: holding her so close and not being able to have her.

Belle woke slowly. Her eyes felt gritty and her limbs heavy, as if she'd been swimming for hours. It took so much energy to open her eyes that she gave up the effort, luxuriating instead in the comfort of just lying there, so utterly relaxed.

It took her some time to realise that it wasn't a bed she lay on. She felt the thrum of a heartbeat under her ear, and, as she moved, the tickle of springy hair under her cheek.

Rafiq! Her head rested on a solid wall of muscle, and pressed against her abdomen lay the hard, flagrant evidence of his arousal.

Her pulse notched up a pace as she remembered all that had happened between them. His deliberate patience and her uncontrolled responses. She'd been like a wild thing, untamed and so blatantly eager for him. Heat washed her cheeks at the memory of her behaviour. It was so unlike her. What must he think of her?

She wriggled, wondering if she could slide off him and away before he woke. If she could face Rafiq when she was fully dressed again, it might be easier. Perhaps then she could pretend that he hadn't stripped her bare of every inhibition, till she'd acted with all the abandon of a sex-mad teenager.

Cautiously she slid down his body a fraction. But the movement only made her more aware of his aroused state, and she paused.

'You are awake, Belle.' His voice was a low rumble that stole her breath.

So much for trying to gather her tattered self-respect unnoticed.

'Yes,' she said, staring at the muscled bicep that lifted in front of her as he raised his hand to stroke her shoulder. His touch was gentle, unassuming, yet to her horror she felt that tingle in her blood that presaged her own readiness. How could it be?

'You are feeling better for your sleep?' he asked, and she nodded.

'Yes, thanks.' She couldn't bring herself to lift her head and look at him. Not yet.

His large hand swooped down her spine, lingered just above her buttocks and slid up again to her shoulder. Belle felt something dip in her stomach at the movement. Her breath caught as she waited for him to repeat the caress.

And when he did she couldn't prevent the involuntary press of her body tight in against him.

Of course he noticed. This time both his large hands slid down, inch by slow inch, past her waist to the dip at the small of her back, then lower, to follow the curve of her buttocks with a heavier touch, pulling her infinitesimally closer. Belle bit down on her lip as the movement brought them together intimately.

'Nevertheless, you must be weary,' he said. 'I shouldn't have tired you so much.'

She grimaced at the way he skirted around what had happened. Perhaps he was shocked by the wanton way she'd behaved. She was!

'I'll get some refreshments for you,' he said, his hands sliding off her.

'No! Not yet, thanks.' If he moved she wouldn't be able to avoid his eyes. At least this way, stupid as it was, she had a respite for a few minutes longer.

'As you wish,' he responded. 'But nevertheless I should move.'

'In a minute,' she urged, spreading her hands across his chest as if her paltry strength could stop him.

'Belle.' This time his voice sounded strained. 'I need to get up.' He curved his fingers round her chin and tilted her face up so she had no option but to meet his gaze.

She wasn't sure what, precisely, she'd expected to see in his face. But it wasn't the obvious tension in his hard-set jaw, or the disturbing glitter in his eyes. He looked like a man in pain.

'Rafiq? What's wrong?'

His lips twisted in a semblance of a smile. 'Nothing that a little distance wouldn't cure.'

The throb of his erection against her abdomen saved further explanation. She'd been so busy dwelling on her own weakness for him, it was a relief to see him affected just as badly.

'Distance isn't the only cure,' she whispered, and saw his eyes widen in surprise.

Then he shook his head. 'Out of the question,' he said. 'I don't want to hurt you. You must already be tender.'

But the longing was clear in his eyes. She guessed it must come close to the expression on her own face as he'd loved her so rapaciously a short time ago. She slipped her hand between them and closed her fingers round him. He pulsed in her hold and she heard him gasp, saw him close his eyes.

'There's no need,' he said roughly.

'I disagree,' she murmured as she pressed a kiss to his heaving chest and pushed herself up. 'I think this is all about need.'

She hoped she could give him at least a fraction of the pleasure he'd given her. The anguished strain on his face as she moved gave her a new boldness, urging her on.

It was the work of a moment to straddle him, positioning herself high above him. His eyes snapped open, his expression a mix of searing anticipation and pained torment that drove her on. Tentatively she lowered herself, her own eyes widening at the sensation of their slow bonding. There was a wonderful completeness about it—a connection between them that was more than physical, she knew. She felt it in every cell of her body, and her heart welled with emotion. Looking down into Rafiq's darkening eyes, she saw that emotion reflected there.

She opened her mouth, so overcome by the sense of oneness that she longed to blurt out the truth. The fact that she loved this man.

But then Rafiq moved, tilting up against her, bringing their union inconceivably closer, tighter, and the words were lost as the spiral of desire spun out of control once more. His hands on her hips, his mouth on her breast, the slow, purposeful drive of his body in concert with her own instinctive moves, rapidly drew her again into that whirlpool of sensation where thought, much less speech, was impossible.

What had begun as an attempt to bring him release became a mutual delight. Rafiq's steady hold kept her from increasing the pace in a race to blind fulfilment. Instead it was a deliberate, exquisite experience of shared pleasure.

Each sensation was spun out to the maximum, made more

potent by the awareness that it was theirs together. The expression in his eyes as they held hers made her heart sing. Her gasp of delight was echoed in his hoarse breathing. As she trembled on the brink of ecstasy she felt his answering tremors grow to shudders. And then the sudden spasm of her fulfilment was matched by the convulsive bucking of his big body as release shattered his control. She called his name, but the sound was lost in the husky flow of Arabic as he groaned out his pleasure.

He reached for her, pulling her down, and Belle subsided onto his chest, hands splayed over his shoulders. It had been cataclysmic, and she needed the safety of his solid strength to centre herself.

Still her body clenched around him, and she felt the hot pulse of his strength deep inside. This elemental proof of his desire for her gave her a surge of primitive pleasure. She felt exhausted, but powerful, dazzled by the sheer potency of their experience and—

'We didn't use protection,' she whispered, suddenly aghast that, in all that had gone before, she hadn't given it a single thought.

How could she have been so reckless? So utterly absorbed in his lovemaking?

'You have nothing to fear, *habibti*.' His deep voice was slurred, and she knew an involuntary stab of delight that she'd affected him so. 'You stand in no danger of illness.' He paused. 'And, knowing you, little one, I cannot believe you are a threat to me, either.'

His hand, warm and soothing, stroked her back in a long, languorous movement. She felt herself relax, despite her concerns.

She nodded. 'You're right. But I'm not using birth control.' It was unlikely she'd conceive so early in her cycle, but the possibility couldn't be ignored. She felt a frisson of emotion, and wondered if it was fear or something else.

There was deep satisfaction in his voice as he replied. 'We're married, Belle. It is natural that we should make children together.' His words hung in the air as his hand, heavily deliberate, slowly circled the curve of her hip.

She should be accustomed to his touch after all they'd done together. But there was something so proprietorial about the way his long fingers caressed her sensitive skin and splayed knowingly over her hipbone. Suddenly she felt very small and defenceless, pressed against his formidable strength.

'Who knows?' he continued, his voice a low burr. 'Even now the miracle of creation may be taking place. I may have planted the seed that will grow into the heir to the throne of Q'aroum.'

His words extinguished the tentative flare of excitement in the pit of her stomach.

She'd felt a trembling anticipation at the idea of carrying a baby, Rafiq's child, inside her, despite the fact that she'd previously had no plans for motherhood. It had felt so *right*, the possibility of being pregnant by him. And his initial words had deepened her secretly burgeoning hope. For an instant she'd been blinded by a vision of them, together, loving parents of an adorable dark-haired baby.

But now she saw that image for what it was: pure fantasy. She'd thought of a child born of love. Rafiq had his sights set only on securing the throne of Q'aroum for another generation. Royal succession. Male primogeniture. That was all it meant to him.

It wasn't the idea of *their* child that thrilled him. It was the possibility of *his* royal heir that filled his voice with smug satisfaction. The legitimate child of the reigning monarch. That was what Rafiq wanted.

She squeezed her eyes tight against the burning hot flood of tears. She would not cry. Not here and now, at any rate. She needed privacy to come to terms with the terrible, ridiculous disappointment that filled her.

Belle began to slide off his big body, intending to curl up on the edge of the massive bed. Even Rafiq, with his obviously virile nature, would understand her need for rest.

But she'd barely moved when his arms wrapped round her, clamping her securely against him.

'I need to sleep,' she lied. She needed to think, to regain some measure of control over her wayward emotions.

'Sleep then.' He sounded like a large cat, purring deep in his throat. She felt the vibration of his yawn deep in his chest.

'I'll just move over—'

'No. Stay where you are. I like having you close against me.'

Despite everything Belle knew a moment of pure delight. But self-preservation was more important. 'I'm too heavy,' she protested.

This time it was his laugh that she felt rippling through his torso. 'Too heavy!' He chuckled. 'You're just perfect, Belle. Now, close your eyes and go to sleep right where you are.'

'But—'

'Or I'll think you're not quite as exhausted as you should be,' he warned, dipping his hand to stroke the side of her breast.

The tingle that spread across her nerve-endings told her everything she needed to know about his dominance over her. She drew a sharp breath and concentrated all her might on not responding to his feather-light caress.

He settled his palm, spreading his fingers wide over her ribs. She heard the heavy thud of his heartbeat, slowly returning to normal, his even breathing, and wondered how long it would be before he slept.

Unbidden, her mind circled back to his words, his satisfaction as he'd spoken of planting his seed, of the all-important heir to his kingdom.

She shouldn't be surprised, she told herself sternly. She'd gone into this marriage with her eyes open. There'd been no pretence that it was anything other than a convenience until the security forces could locate the would-be coup leaders. And Rafiq had made it plain that he saw no need to abstain from the perks of marriage, even though his heart wasn't engaged. They were married, he'd said, so of course they would sleep together. And, went his irrefutable logic, if they slept together it was natural that pregnancy would be the outcome.

She couldn't blame him, much as she wanted to. He'd married her for the sake of his country. He was an honourable man. He'd even risked his own life to save hers, and had courted the scorn of his people by paying that stupefying ransom. He hadn't lied or made promises he wouldn't keep.

And what could she expect, after all? He was the Royal Prince in a largely traditional state, reared from birth to believe in his own superior authority. Of course he'd see nothing wrong in bedding his own wife. Or finding pleasure when it was so freely available.

The fault lay with her. For being swept up against her better judgement into a situation she should have avoided. For walking right into this mess.

She'd talked herself into it. She'd pretended it was for the sake of Q'aroum, and the people she'd come to like so much in her weeks here. For the sake of Rafiq, fearlessly facing terrorist threats in his attempt to retain peace in his country. For the sake of her debt to him. She owed him her life. If he hadn't arrived on the island when he had she knew both she and Duncan would have died, either of dehydration or of injuries in the cyclone.

But the truth was simpler. She'd married him for love. Despite the logic that told her it would be a recipe for disaster, she'd given herself to the man she adored. The strong, honourable, protective, determined man who'd completely stolen her common sense. She'd foolishly hoped that, once married, he'd come to reciprocate that love.

She'd wanted a fairytale ending.

Just now, in the throes of passion, she'd almost admitted out loud her feelings for him. She cringed at how close she'd come to total embarrassment. In her stupid, lovesick way, she'd even imagined he returned her feelings, that what they'd shared was possible only because it was love they felt, not lust.

And because of her stupidity she hadn't considered the possibility of a child born of this union. A child whose parents were linked only by legalities, not love.

Rafiq waited till he was sure Belle slept, then rolled her onto her side and drew a light cover over her. She must be exhausted, so deeply did she sleep. He reached out a hand and stroked the fine honey-gold strands of hair back from her face. There was a red mark on her neck, and another near her collarbone. He'd been too rough. He hadn't considered how easily her soft skin might bruise.

His gaze moved from the mark up to her mouth. Her lips were swollen, heavy from the pressure of his. He'd need to be careful in future, more restrained. When he'd finally taken her he'd simply lost control, absorbed in the wondrous exhilaration of making love to her.

His body stirred with the knowledge that she was his now, irrevocably. There would be many more times like this. A lifetime in which to try and sate his desire for her.

He clenched his hand against the need to reach out and touch her, caress her awake and make love to her again. His gaze roved her features. Her cool, classical beauty might tempt a man into believing she was distant and controlled. But her mouth gave her away, he decided smugly, remembering the feel of her lips against his as she gasped her fulfilment. She had a mouth that told its own story of her hot-blooded, passionate nature.

And she was all his. This delicate, vibrant, adorable woman

who had the determination and sheer guts of ten men. Who took natural disasters and kidnap in her stride. Who was unfazed by the vast pomp of a Q'aroumi royal wedding with its throng of onlookers. She'd treated his people just as she should, with a restrained but real welcome that had already endeared her to many, as had her halting but effective greetings in their own language.

She'd even faced down Dawud with his own dagger!

Rafiq felt his chest swell with pride as he looked down at her. She would make Q'aroum a perfect queen.

She would make him the perfect wife.

He slid out of bed and padded across the carpet, searching for discarded clothes. She needed rest, and if he stayed here any longer it was all too possible he'd throw his good intentions to the winds and wake her for more sex.

The trouble was that once the idea had surfaced of her being pregnant with his child the possibility had consumed him. He imagined her belly swollen with their baby. He'd developed a covetous streak a mile wide since meeting her, and he knew that bearing his child would bind her to him more securely than even the legal and moral promises that joined them. And he wanted that. Wanted the certainty of having her forever at his side.

He'd been so caught up in the thrill of the moment he hadn't spared a thought for the fact that she might not feel ready for motherhood. That it would have been wiser to bide his time and sound her out on the subject.

Rafiq pulled on his trousers and pushed the hair back from his face. He'd have to be more cautious in future.

He strolled to the tent's entrance and stood in the cool shadows, staring out at the view he knew and loved so well. It felt absolutely right to be here with Belle. For a moment he allowed himself to wish that his grandfather were still alive, to meet her and see what a wonderful prize his grandson had won for himself.

He stretched, satisfied and pleasantly relaxed. His gaze followed the flight of a falcon, wheeling high over the edge of the desert. Below it a hill of sand curved steeply down to the oasis, its pristine slope marred by the tracks of several horses.

Immediately Rafiq tensed, his mind racing. He and Belle had ridden in from the north, not the east, and when they'd arrived there had been no other tracks. The security check this morning had been by air, with the helicopter landing in its usual spot, just behind where the tent now stood.

The hairs on his neck stood on end as the implications struck him, and instantly he moved into the shadows, away from the opening. The armed forces' security personnel assigned to guard him and Belle were out there, of course. With Selim still at large he wouldn't have taken her into the desert alone. The soldiers had come by four-wheel drive and were stationed at strategic locations around the oasis, so as not to disturb the privacy of their sheikh. Fleetingly he wondered about the fate of those guards assigned to protection duty. None of them would have willingly admitted intruders.

Whoever had come by horse had somehow passed through that security cordon. His jaw hardened at the sure knowledge of who they must be.

At any other time he'd welcome the opportunity to get his hands on Selim's fat neck. But not now. Not with Belle here.

If anything should happen to her…

CHAPTER TWELVE

'BELLE.' For an instant his lips met hers, coaxing her out of sleep. Then his voice came, soft yet urgent in her ear, his hand warm on her cheek. 'Quickly and quietly. You must get up. There's danger.'

Her eyes snapped open at his compelling tone. She blinked dazedly into his eyes, but already he'd drawn back, pulling her into a sitting position.

Before she could open her mouth to question, his palm slid to cover her mouth. 'Not a sound,' he whispered. 'We're in danger, and you must do as I say. Do you understand?'

She read the grim lines bracketing his mouth, the steely determination in his gaze, and knew with an instant plummeting sensation of dread that her worst nightmare had come true. Fear prickled her neck as she thought of the merciless men who'd abducted her and left her to die. Who'd set off a bomb in a crowded city.

Shakily she nodded.

For a moment longer his eyes held hers, the unguarded emotion she saw there stealing her breath, making her pulse race. Then it was gone as his face settled into a mask of formidable purpose.

'Here.' He pressed something into her hands as he moved away. 'Cover yourself.'

Her legs trembled as she slid off the bed, her hands fumbling nervelessly as she struggled with the garment, eventually identifying it as Rafiq's discarded shirt. Ridiculous to feel such relief as the fine cotton drifted down around her, covering her to her thighs. Mere cloth was no barrier against the pain those renegades could inflict. But she drew it gratefully round herself, as if the fact that it was Rafiq's could protect her.

She'd only managed to do up a few buttons when she heard it. A muted sound from just outside.

Her head jerked round and she met Rafiq's steady gaze. He was whispering into what looked like a walkie-talkie, and as she watched he stooped and hid it under a corner of carpet.

Then he was striding across to her, taking her shoulders in his hands.

'Help is on its way, little one. No matter what happens, remember that. Meanwhile, we must play for time.'

'Rafiq,' she whispered, suddenly desperate at the knowledge that they might not survive whatever lurked outside the tent. That all she felt for him was still unsaid. 'I—'

A burst of guttural Arabic from the doorway cut her off as a crowd of armed men burst in. Rafiq stepped in front of her, shielding her, and she realised with a horror that paralysed her vocal cords that she knew them.

The scrawny one with the malicious smile. And the towering giant, with his brawny hand grasping a long-bladed knife. She'd never forget him. He was the one who'd broken Duncan's leg as easily as snapping a twig. She stared up into his cold eyes and shivered as a flood of nausea swamped her. She pressed a trembling hand against Rafiq's back, as if she could absorb some of his strength.

'What do you want, Selim?' Rafiq cut across whatever their leader was saying. 'Have you come to pay your respects to your sheikh?'

The man he addressed gaped for a moment, eyes wide in his pudgy face. Then he drew his lips into a snarling line and took a step closer. His entourage crowded beside him. Belle realised now that there were only four of them. Still enough to overpower Rafiq and herself far too easily. Especially as they were unarmed.

Selim spoke again, a belligerent flow of words she had no hope of understanding. But there was no need for translation. Their situation was clear, and all too hopeless. This had to be Rafiq's kinsman, the man who'd masterminded her kidnap and the other recent acts of violence in the hope of destabilising Q'aroum's government and grabbing power for himself.

She looked at his smug expression, the signs of dissipation on his fleshy countenance, and shivered. Here was a man who'd be utterly ruthless in pursuit of his own ends.

'Ah, yes,' said Rafiq coolly, once more interrupting his cousin. 'A transfer of power. And how much more convincing it would be if I were alive and apparently willing to participate.'

Selim smiled then, with all the charm of an alligator watching its next meal. He obviously liked the sound of his own voice, Belle decided, as he held the floor again. And that self-satisfied smirk sent a shiver of apprehension down her spine. It looked just as lethal as the weapons his henchmen brandished.

Wretchedly she wondered how long it would be before the help Rafiq had promised would arrive. Each second dragged with excruciating slowness. It seemed a lifetime since this group had burst in on them, but common sense told her it couldn't be more than a couple of minutes.

Play for time. That was what Rafiq had said. That must be why he was encouraging his cousin to talk.

But unfortunately Selim was no fool. The realisation had no sooner surfaced in her mind than he was gesturing to his followers that it was time to go. One of them left the tent and the other two stepped forward, one towards Rafiq and the other, the hulking brute whose bruise she'd worn for so long, coming for her, his eyes alight with sadistic satisfaction. Involuntarily she caught her breath, and pressed closer to Rafiq.

He shifted his weight, half turning so that he faced the giant who was reaching for her. He said something in his native tongue with a soft deadliness that brought her kidnapper to a startled halt. Then she saw the speculation in the other man's eyes, and a glitter of excitement that made her heart sink.

'We will go with you,' Rafiq added in English. 'But no one touches my wife.'

For an instant the tableau held. Over Rafiq's rigid shoulder she saw the three men frozen in place, an automatic reaction to the commanding hauteur of his words. Then Selim spat out something short and vulgar enough to make his bully-boys snigger, and the big one reached out a long arm towards her.

There was a sudden swift movement. Rafiq stepped forward to meet him, and the next thing she knew the other man was on his knees, clutching his midriff.

There was a hiss of comment from his comrade, who lifted his handgun to point it directly at Rafiq, and Belle shouted out a hoarse warning.

'Quiet, bitch,' Selim snarled in accented English. 'One scream from you and you'll see your precious husband die before your eyes.'

Belle had no doubt he meant it. Nausea welled in her throat as her gaze flicked from his ruthless expression to the gun pointed at Rafiq. There was nothing she could do. Nothing but wait and watch this drama play out, praying that they'd both survive.

The tall man rose to his feet with a lurch and a grunt, and suddenly she knew just how unlikely it was that they'd survive. There was murder in his eyes as he looked at her husband.

Selim snapped out an order, but the other man didn't react.

Instead he drew himself up to his full, enormous height and lifted the curved knife in his hand.

'Rafiq!' Her anguished whisper was drowned by Selim, as he barked another command to his sidekick. But it was too late. The big man was circling, one hand gripping his dagger as he focussed on Rafiq.

Dread welled in her. There was only one way this could end. Strong and powerful as Rafiq was, he'd be no match for a man built like the side of a house. A man, moreover, armed with a wicked blade, when Rafiq had no weapon and no shield.

The seconds ticked by in agonising slowness as the two men faced off. Then, without warning, there was a flurry of movement. They closed together and she saw the blade arc down with deadly intent. She couldn't prevent a gasp of sheer horror as she watched the point aim for Rafiq's heart. But once more he somehow shifted his weight at the right moment, toppling his adversary and falling with him to the floor. For a moment Rafiq was on top, his whole body straining against the power of the man below him. Then, abruptly, their situations were reversed, and it was Selim's crony using his full weight to subdue Rafiq.

Frantic, Belle swung round, surveying the tent for something she could use as a weapon. But the icebox was too heavy, and she could hardly batter the goon with a cushion.

There was a loud thump, followed by a hiss of indrawn breath, and she spun back to see them tumbling together, rolling across the floor. As they moved she saw, barely visible against the stained-glass colours of the carpets, a trail of bright blood.

The two men, locked in a merciless embrace, heaved together near her feet. She heard a dreadful cracking, as if of bone on bone, and remembered, sickeningly, the way this brutal attacker had broken Duncan's leg. She'd never felt more helpless, more utterly useless than now, as she watched the man she loved battle against unwinnable odds for his life.

She was trying to anticipate the next move of their writhing bodies, intending to throw herself on Rafiq's attacker, when she saw the pair of them jerk, heard a low moan, and felt all the blood rush from her head as she knew the worst had happened.

Belle stared at the abruptly still tangle of bodies on the floor, and knew that when they separated everything would change for ever. She tried to imagine a world without Rafiq filling her life. But her mind rebelled, refusing to accept such an impossible reality. Numbly she stood, barely aware of the tremors that racked her body, waiting for the inevitable.

Endless seconds passed before there was any sign of life. Aghast, her mouth filled with the metallic taste of despair, she watched as the bodies heaved, limbs scrabbling. She squeezed her eyes shut, postponing the moment she dreaded.

He's dead, she told herself. But still the words made no sense. Her brain refused to accept it.

She heard Selim burst into rapid speech. But she was so overcome it took her a moment to realise he sounded shocked, not satisfied.

'Belle.' It was Rafiq's soft whisper that snapped her eyes open.

He was on his knees, blood streaming from a wound at his side, his throat reddened with the imprint of large, encircling fingers. He swayed unsteadily as he staggered to his feet.

And on the floor beside him lay his attacker, sprawled on his stomach. A telltale pool of blood spread out from beneath him across the fine silk carpets.

'Rafiq!' It was a strangled sob, her voice choked by the raw emotions that constricted her throat. She took a step towards him, her arms outstretched. And out of the corner of her eye she saw movement. It was Selim's other henchman, raising his gun slowly, deliberately, to aim at Rafiq.

'No!' Belle flung herself forward, knocking Rafiq off balance. There was an explosion of deafening sound, and the world spun away into searing blackness.

CHAPTER THIRTEEN

WEARILY Belle surveyed the familiar hospital room. What a co-incidence that they'd put her in the same room. *Déjà-vu*. Only this time she wasn't nearly so eager to leave.

Last time she'd wanted to escape the fussy hospital routine and get on with her life, eager to put the trauma of abduction behind her. She'd been sure that immersing herself in work would be the perfect antidote to the stress she'd been through.

Her lips twisted in a sad smile. How differently things had worked out. Now she'd be leaving the quiet safety of her hospital bed not as a nine-day wonder, a foreign marine archaeologist who'd been held to ransom, but as the wife of Sheikh Rafiq Kamil Ibn Makram al Akhtar, Sovereign Prince of Q'aroum.

Her destiny wasn't her own any more. It was inextricably bound to Rafiq and to his country.

Somewhere deep inside her rose a tiny bubble of emotion. So deep she couldn't identify it. She wondered if she should feel excited or pleased—maybe even nervous about what the future held. But she felt nothing. Or almost nothing. It was as if she'd been sealed into a cocoon, separated from everyone else by an invisible barrier. One that somehow obliterated the stronger emotions that she knew she should be experiencing.

She supposed it was shock. Or maybe she'd just given up worrying about what she couldn't control.

There'd been that flash of overwhelming relief right at the beginning, when she'd opened her eyes to see a white-coated medical team and a doctor assuring her, each time she asked, that His Highness would live. The knife-thrust had missed his ribs and vital organs. Rafiq was safe. She'd closed her eyes and drifted back into unconsciousness as the words sank in.

When she'd woken again she had felt as if she'd been run over by a truck, taped so tight she could barely breathe. But the miraculous news of Rafiq's survival had overridden her discomfort. And, with the news that the gunshot wound to her shoulder would heal after careful treatment, she should have been on top of the world.

All the medical staff had told her how lucky she was. Dawud too, each time he'd visited, had referred to her courage and her good fortune. And, of course, her mum, being a nurse, had understood exactly what all the medical jargon meant, and had reiterated over the long-distance line that Belle was luckier than she had any right to be after throwing herself in front of a bullet.

So why was it she felt nothing?

She sighed and let her gaze roam across the lavish collection of flowers adorning the long shelf beside the window. Her attention was drawn, as always, to the waxy beauty of the deep-throated, exotic orchids that had been so reverentially placed by the nurse at the front. 'A gift from His Highness,' she'd murmured.

Rafiq.

Belle's lips firmed and she turned away. She'd seen him twice since the shooting. The first time she'd woken he'd been there, though she hadn't seen him immediately, as the medical staff crowded round. But as the doctor had assured her that the Sheikh would live, Rafiq himself had shouldered his way forward and grasped her hand. She remembered the intensity of his fathoms-deep eyes, and the lingering warmth of his hold against her fingers as she'd fallen again into the swirling darkness.

And the second time had been just last night. He'd looked harsher than she'd ever seen him. His brows drawn in a straight dark line and his mouth bracketed by slashing grooves. For a moment, as he'd walked in the door, her heart had leapt; she'd felt heat rise in her cheeks and her pulse thud faster. But her joy had drained away as he'd looked at her with shuttered eyes. He hadn't reached for her, but had stood back from the bed, hands clasped behind him. He hadn't even taken a seat, but had stood, his expression unreadable, just out of reach.

Not that she'd have stretched her arm out to touch him—not after that first instant of unguarded emotion. Not when he'd looked at her like a polite stranger and spoken in neutral tones about her upcoming release from hospital and plans for her mother to fly over from Australia.

He'd spoken directly to her, yet somehow he'd managed to avoid meeting her eyes.

Something inside her had shrivelled up and died as she'd watched him. She'd realised then at last, with a cool, clear logic that was irrefutable, just how foolish her dreams of shared love had been.

It had been an arranged marriage. She had never been Rafiq's choice, just a necessary part of a political manoeuvre.

Listening to his cool, unemotional voice describe how the conspirators had been captured when the armed forces had stormed the oasis, and inform her that their trials had already been scheduled in the high court, Belle had realised just where she stood. The circumstances that had forced their marriage no longer existed.

He didn't need her any more.

She'd spent the night sleepless, wondering about the Q'aroumi laws on divorce.

'Belle.' She started, horrified to discover that even through the bubble of her emotional vacuum his voice had the power to stir her.

She raised her eyes and there he was, just as breath-stealingly handsome as ever. The traditional robes he wore emphasised his aura of power, and his aloofness. For an instant she let herself remember him, glossy hair spilling across his broad, bare shoulders, desire lighting the depths of his green eyes. Then she slammed the lid on such foolishness. It had been an aberration. A few hours that had meant everything to her, but nothing to him. Now she had to put the memory of it behind her.

'Hello, Rafiq. Have you come to take me to the palace?' Her voice was calm, lightly enquiring.

He paused in mid-step, his eyes boring into hers. 'I am your husband. Who else would escort you home?'

Of course. It was his duty. And Rafiq never shirked his duty. Not even if it meant sacrificing his future, and hers, to a loveless marriage.

She opened her mouth to say the palace wasn't home. Not to her at least. Then closed her mouth. There was no point in being childish about it.

'Are you ready to leave?' he asked, as he walked around to the back of her wheelchair.

Automatically her gaze strayed to the window shelf. 'The flowers...' Silly how it was his orchids she focussed on, not the bright lilies sent by her mum and Rosalie, nor the massed bouquets from other well-wishers.

'They'll be sent on,' he said from behind her. And then he pushed the chair towards the door.

A sudden, urgent pang of something like fear slashed through her at the thought of leaving this sanctuary to be alone with Rafiq. But that was stupid. She lifted her chin and managed a smile for the nurse who held open the door for them. And more smiles and thanks for the other staff who waited in the foyer to see them off.

Above her, Rafiq's deep voice thanked them all for their care. And then they were heading out, under the *port cochère,* to the waiting limousine.

Belle had her feet on the ground, ready to stand, when Rafiq bent low and lifted her into his arms.

'Rafiq! You shouldn't—your injury.'

She caught the flare of something bright and compelling in his eyes as he looked down at her. The heat of his body penetrated the chill that encompassed her, and surreptitiously she inhaled his evocative scent. A nervous tremor raced through her.

'I'm fine, Belle. Well enough to carry my wife.'

His wife. It was as if he had to keep reminding himself of his duty.

She tightened her jaw and looked away, to the open car door and the chauffeur standing to attention there.

She felt the deep breath Rafiq drew, his chest expanding against her, his fingers curling tighter. Then he strode to the car and deposited her on the back seat. She shifted into the corner, hunching away from him as he joined her. Amazingly, she'd forgotten how vibrant his presence was, how it invaded her space.

The trip to the palace should only have taken fifteen minutes, but the roads were lined with people and the driver kept their speed to a crawl.

'Do you think you can manage a smile?' Rafiq murmured as he lifted his hand in greeting, responding to the cheers and waves of the crowd. 'Some of these people have been here for hours, waiting to catch a glimpse of you.'

'Of me?' She swung round to stare at him.

'Of course.' He turned from his open window, and the intensity of his expression seared into her very being. 'You are a national heroine, Belle. Saviour of the Royal Prince. Every man, woman and child in Q'aroum has heard the story of how the beautiful young bride of the Sheikh threw herself in front of an armed assassin to save the life of her husband.'

There was a harsh note in his voice that she couldn't identify. A starkly repressed emotion that nagged, just below the surface of his carefully composed features. It made her shiver.

'What nonsense,' she said.

'It's the truth,' he interjected, his voice deep enough to stir her senses in unwanted feminine response. 'You saved my life. Even though it could have cost you yours.'

His gaze held hers, and she felt the potency, the sheer power of his personality, and of the emotions he kept so strictly tethered.

'That single act of foolish bravery seems to have convinced even the staunchest traditionalist that I was incredibly clever to take you as my wife.'

Belle caught her breath. Finally she let it ease out of her, deflated to realise that for a moment she'd waited for him to say he was glad he'd married her, but for the most personal of reasons.

Disappointment shafted, keen as a knife, into her chest.

Stupid, stupid woman.

She turned towards her own window, and this time she raised her arm to the people who thronged close, waving and cheering. But she couldn't return their smiles.

Rafiq watched her from the corner of his eye and wondered again if he'd done right to bring her home from the hospital today. The doctor had warned that she was in shock, though the gunshot wound was healing well. He'd suggested waiting. But Rafiq had been adamant. She needed to come home now her condition was stable. Belle would have nursing staff on hand at the palace to give her twenty-four-hour care.

He stifled an upsurge of intense nausea at the thought of her injury, and once more thrust aside the image that still crowded his brain in every unguarded moment. Of Belle, unconscious in his arms, the lifeblood pumping out of her. Of him, utterly helpless, as he alternately cajoled and threatened her insensate form into staying alive.

He felt the coldness clamp round his heart again, knowing how close he'd come to losing her. And all because of his selfish plan to win her, coax her into trusting him enough to become his wife in reality as well as name. How could he have been so stupid as to take such a chance with her when Selim was still at large?

No matter that his security advisors had assured him the oasis trip would be safe. He should have known. He should have kept her securely at the hunting lodge till it was all over. He should have kept her under armed guard at all times. He'd failed her when she'd needed him most.

He'd never felt as useless, as worthless, as when he'd thought he'd lost her. That she'd done something as unforgivably ridiculous as offer her life for his overwhelmed him with guilt.

He wasn't worthy of her.

It was his fault she'd been hurt. His fault that now she held herself with the wary distance of the shell-shocked. It had been one trauma for her after another. And it was all down to him.

Bleakly he wondered if he'd have the strength to grant her the freedom she so obviously desired. By anyone's reckoning she deserved it.

When the car pulled up at the palace entrance a crowd of servants spilled out, one of them pushing a wheelchair for her. But Rafiq moved first, alighting from the car and scooping her up into his arms, where she belonged. She was warm, and frighteningly fragile. Careful of her sling, he held her close and breathed deeply, absorbing the fresh, unique scent of her skin.

It felt so right, holding her. As long as he ignored the cool query in her eyes and the tension emanating from her taut body, signalling that she'd rather be anywhere than in his arms.

He strode through the wide entrance to find Dawud waiting for them, a large, unmistakable leather case in his hands.

'Madam.' Dawud bowed to Belle. 'I am pleased to welcome you home.'

'Thank you, Dawud.' Her voice was too high-pitched to be natural, but she was calm. Too calm in the circumstances, Rafiq decided.

'My wife is tired, Dawud,' he said brusquely. 'We'll deal with that later.' He nodded to the case. 'When she's rested.'

'I'm not tired,' she objected, in that high, tight voice that was so unlike her natural warm tones. 'What's in the box?'

'Nothing that can't wait,' Rafiq muttered, turning away towards the corridor.

'Dawud?' Belle asked. 'What's this about?'

'It's a matter of tradition, Highness,' Dawud said, following them. 'When the Sheikh weds it's customary for him to appear before his people and for his bride to wear—'

'The Peacock's Eye,' Belle interjected, turning her eyes to meet his. 'You got it back?'

Rafiq stared down at her, wishing he could discern a spark of pleasure or excitement in her at the prospect of having such fabled gems for her own. Anything but the cool reserve that kept her so remote.

He nodded. 'It was retrieved yesterday.'

'Well, I suppose I'd better wear it,' she said, with a total lack of enthusiasm. 'We don't want to stand in the way of tradition. It's your duty, after all.'

Rafiq frowned, sure he heard sarcasm in her tone. But her look was bland. What wouldn't he give to have the *real* Belle in his arms: feisty, passionate, so *alive*.

'Very well,' He turned and strode towards the throne room. 'Let's get this over with. Come, Dawud.'

Belle stared at the jewelled necklace, stunned, as anyone would be, at the sheer, inconceivable magnificence of it. The array of gemstones must be worth several kings' ransoms. The weight of gold was enormous, and the exquisite artisanship almost beyond belief.

Rafiq had given this up for her? It seemed incredible. But then she remembered. He hadn't done it for her; he'd done it to keep his kingdom from international opprobrium.

Her gaze swung from the sparkling necklace, revealed on its bed of dark velvet, to his face, looming above her. He wore his shuttered look still—no way of knowing what he was thinking.

Nevertheless, the enormity of his action left her speechless. How many men would have made that decision to save the lives of strangers by paying this ransom?

'You may go, Dawud,' Rafiq said, his tone sharp. 'Have the chamberlain announce that we'll be there shortly. But not for long. My wife needs rest.'

'The people will understand, Your Highness.' Dawud bowed and left the room.

'You're sure about this, Belle?' Rafiq asked.

She nodded. Best to get it over as quickly as possible.

Maybe she *was* exhausted after all. For suddenly the comfortable numbness was wearing off. She felt a tearing sensation deep inside, as if the pain she'd warded off for so long ripped at her from within. And it was getting harder and harder to remain calm and detached now Rafiq was so close.

'Very well.' She watched as he lifted the necklace from its case, saw the way the light reflected off the enormous gems and swallowed hard.

He stood behind her and lowered it over her head. He

brushed her hair aside and snicked the heavy clasp closed. Belle felt the weight of it like a yoke around her neck and drew a deep, calming breath. Suddenly she didn't feel like Belle Winters any more.

She looked up and into the antique mirror on the other side of the salon. There was Rafiq, tall and handsome behind her. And, sitting before him, there she was, unrecognisable now as a mere hard-working marine archaeologist. Transformed by the remarkable jewelled necklace into someone altogether different.

Even with her arm in a sling, and wearing her ordinary clothes, she'd subtly changed. It had to be the awesome beauty of the jewellery that did it.

She frowned. No, it was more than that. She felt different. As if the collar was imbued with the weight of all those centuries of tradition. As if she was, indeed, the true bride of a prince.

She blinked at her suddenly blurry reflection, letting herself wish again, one last time, that there was love between her and Rafiq. That, like one of his ancestors, he'd abducted her off the high seas out of pure covetousness, out of personal desire. Not for mere public show.

'Don't cry, *habibti.*' His voice sounded hoarse, but her vision was too blurred now for her to make out his expression in the mirror. Her throat stung with the sharp pain of grief as she fought to repress a sob.

'Belle.' His hand brushed her cheek, and then he was hunkering down before her, gathering her hands into his. 'My sweet Belle, it's all been too much for you. We'll postpone this till you're better.'

Furiously she blinked, trying to dam the welling tears. 'No. Let's get this show over with. Give the people the fairytale they want and be done with it.' She didn't bother to hide her bitterness.

Silence.

'You misunderstand,' he said at last, in a cool, toneless voice.

'The giving of the Peacock's Eye is not for display. It's not to satisfy the curiosity of the populace, though the tradition is that once it's given it will be shown to the people.'

She stared down at his long fingers, now grasping hers. Did he know how tightly he held them?

'Belle!'

She jerked her head up and met his gaze. And immediately she felt a slow, tingling warmth sizzle in her veins. That look in his eyes...

'Even in the days when the Sheikh kept a harem the Eye was bestowed only on his favourite. The mistress of his heart,' Rafiq explained, his voice dropping to a velvety murmur. 'And since those days times have changed. I told you—the men of my family have for generations taken only one wife. The al Akhtars are famous in the region for many things, including the constancy of their affections.'

She stared into his eyes and saw a blaze of heat there that made her breath catch.

'The Eye is given to each new bride as a symbol of her place in her husband's heart.' He bent his head and kissed, first one hand, then the other.

'Heart of my heart. Flesh of my flesh,' he whispered, drawing her hand to rest over the rapid, heavy thud of his heart that matched her own. 'I give you the Eye as I could never give it to another. You are mine, Belle, no matter the circumstances that brought us together.'

It was only the grasp of his hand round her wrist, the sizzling heat of his body beneath her touch, that convinced her this was real. Not some fantasy.

She opened her mouth, but her throat closed on whatever words she'd hoped to find. He dropped to his knees before her, leaning close so that he was only a breath away.

'I love you, Belle. That is why the Eye belongs to you. You

are my woman, my wife, my love. Feel how my heart beats for you, *habibti*. You are everything to me.' He pressed her hand to his chest and she felt the tumultuous thump of his heart.

Her soul was soaring, taking flight with the joyous possibility of hope.

Rafiq loved her. She tried to take it in, to accept it, but reality intervened. She tugged her hand away, but he wouldn't release it, held it tight against him.

'That's not true,' she whispered, even though saying it out loud was agony. 'You married me to keep Q'aroum safe, so you wouldn't lose face before your people…' Her words trailed off as she watched his lips curve up in a self-satisfied smile.

'So my advisors suggested, little one. But do you really think I would marry any woman other than the one I want for life? Do you not think I'd have been able to deal with the tawdry ambitions of Selim and his crew?'

Belle stared into his arrogantly satisfied face. Saw the possessive light in his eyes and almost believed. How she *wanted* to believe.

'But the risk was too great,' she protested. 'Selim was organising terrorist attacks.' She shook her head, struggling to understand. 'And then last night you were so distant, as if you regretted being stuck with me.' She couldn't keep the hurt out of her voice.

He shook his head, as if despairing of her naïvety. 'I'm glad my arguments were so convincing, my sweet. But, believe me, I don't need to hide behind my wife, no matter how brave and beautiful she is, in order to rule my kingdom.'

And there it was. Suddenly, undeniably. Convincing her as nothing else had. The arrogant cast of his features, the haughty tilt of his head, the proud, strong jut of his chin that bespoke generations of autocratic power. Rafiq al Akhtar was a man who could rule Q'aroum alone if he chose, following the traditions of his forebears, assured in his right as born leader. Of course his people would follow where he led. But he'd chosen the path of democracy.

And he'd chosen her.

The knowledge stole her breath. A slow, delicious sensation, like hope unfurling in her chest, sent warmth tingling through her. She gulped down a choking sob of unbelievable emotion.

'And as for being distant, little tigress, it was guilt at putting you at risk that made me hold back. To have the woman you love offer her life for you is a humbling experience. A shattering one to any man of feeling.' His gaze held hers, so she read tension and, for the first time, vulnerability in his expression. There was agony in his eyes. Such as she'd never seen before.

'You'd gone through so much already, and all because of me,' he continued, his voice hoarse with emotion. 'I was afraid that this time it was too much, that even a woman of your spirit must finally call enough. That you would blame me, as you had every right to do, and turn your face from me.'

She gazed at him, almost fearing to believe her ears.

'Belle!' His grip tightened and she saw a shadow cross his face, betraying a pain she'd never guessed at. 'Say that you understand! That you know how I feel.'

She'd never thought to hear him sound desperate. It ravaged her heart to recognise such pain in him. 'Rafiq, I—'

'You must, Belle. I cannot hear anything else from you. I've wrestled with my conscience, but I cannot give you up.'

His eyes blazed fire, his brows furrowed, and the pulse at the base of his throat betrayed the extremity of his emotions.

She slipped her hand from his death-grip and lifted it, trembling, to his face. His jaw clenched hard under her touch, and his nostrils flared as she settled her palm on his warm skin.

'Just as well,' she whispered brokenly. 'Because I never want to leave you, Rafiq.'

For one long, glorious moment his gaze held hers, and she felt as if she really could do anything in the world—even fly. For nothing, ever, in the history of all the ages, could surpass this wondrous delight.

'You love me?' His voice was raw.

'I love you.' To admit it out loud was bliss, almost as perfect as hearing him say it. She leaned towards him, but he was too quick. It was his mouth swooping down on hers, his arms cradling her tenderly against him. And she fell into him gratefully, knowing she was coming home.

Time stood still as they found solace and peace in each other's arms. They were one at last, and it was perfect.

Finally, reluctantly, Belle opened her eyes as he drew back a fraction. There was open adoration in Rafiq's gaze. Her heart skipped a beat and she knew that, however many years they'd share, she'd always melt when he looked at her like that.

'Your shoulder,' he murmured.

'It's fine,' she said. 'What about your ribs?'

'A scratch.' He grinned. 'Right now I feel as if I could take on the world and win.'

'Then you can help me face those crowds outside.'

'You've no need to worry, *habibti*. They're halfway to adoring you already. I told you—my people, *our* people, are romantics at heart.'

Belle hoped he was right. She had so much to learn about her new home. She wanted to make Rafiq proud of her.

'After all, they must know by now that I'm besotted with you. I've made my feelings all too obvious to everyone—except, it seems, the woman I love.'

She smiled, secure now in the knowledge that her dream really had come true.

'Even Dawud knew,' Rafiq said, as he lifted her hand to his lips and pressed a kiss against each finger.

'Sorry?' She couldn't think when he touched her like that.

'That old devil Dawud,' Rafiq explained. 'I didn't ask him to get out the Peacock's Eye today. He took it upon himself. He'd never do that unless he was absolutely sure of my love for you.'

'Does it matter so much?' she teased.

He shook his head and swept her up for another kiss. 'All that matters is that you're mine, of your own free will.'

And when they eventually appeared on the balcony, much, much later, the patient crowd could see beyond question that tradition had been upheld. The Peacock's Eye had been bestowed upon the woman who held their prince's heart.

4 FREE

BOOKS AND A SURPRISE GIFT!

We would like to take this opportunity to thank you for reading this Mills & Boon® book by offering you the chance to take FOUR more specially selected titles from the Modern Romance™ series absolutely FREE! We're also making this offer to introduce you to the benefits of the Mills & Boon® Reader Service™—

- ★ **FREE home delivery**
- ★ **FREE gifts and competitions**
- ★ **FREE monthly Newsletter**
- ★ **Exclusive Reader Service offers**
- ★ **Books available before they're in the shops**

Accepting these FREE books and gift places you under no obligation to buy, you may cancel at any time, even after receiving your free shipment. Simply complete your details below and return the entire page to the address below. You don't even need a stamp!

YES! Please send me 4 free Modern Romance books and a surprise gift. I understand that unless you hear from me, I will receive 6 superb new titles every month for just £2.89 each, postage and packing free. I am under no obligation to purchase any books and may cancel my subscription at any time. The free books and gift will be mine to keep in any case.

P7ZED

Ms/Mrs/Miss/Mr ....Initials ....

BLOCK CAPITALS PLEASE

Surname ....

Address ....

....

....Postcode.............................

Send this whole page to:
UK: FREEPOST CN8I, Croydon, CR9 3WZ